BURNING EMBERS

A dragon anthology

It all begins with fire...

BURNING EMBERS

A dragon anthology

By the members of
The Richmond Fantasy Collective

Cover and Title Copyright © 2023 by Richmond Fantasy Collective
Stories Edited by Claire Bradshaw
Cover Art by Yael Nava
Interior Art by Caroline Branch

Introduction © 2023 by Richmond Fantasy Collective
DAUGHTER of FIRE © 2023 by Kaitlyn Reeds
WHAT IF IT KILLS YOUR DRAGON? © 2023 by Renee Hill
TERMINAL FREIGHT © 2023 by Dean Radt
DRAGON'S CLUTCH © 2023 by Valerie Brown
TALES for YOUNG DRAGONS © 2023 by Ivy Hamid

July 2024

Richmond, Virginia

ISBN 979-8-9894917-1-1 (paperback)
ISBN 979-8-9894917-0-4 (ebook)

Published in the United States of America.

ACKNOWLEDGEMENTS

We thank you for picking up this anthology. Our group, the Richmond Fantasy Collective, first gathered five years ago, following a James River Writer's conference. Since then we've been getting to know one another, developing new projects, and helping each other hone our craft. This anthology has been a year-long project for the Collective, and we hope it entertains you. We also want to thank James River Writers, our friends, our families, and the professionals who helped us produce this work.

We invite you to follow our journey on Instagram **@rfcwriters**.

Valerie Brown
Ivy Hamid
Renée Hill
Dean Radt
Kaitlyn Reeds

CONTENTS

I

Daughter of Fire

Kaitlyn Reeds

Burning embers were all that remained of her mother's letter after the flames engulfed it. Neri dropped the ashes onto the stone floor and stomped on them with her boot for good measure. She hissed through gritted teeth and dug her heel into the ashes one last time before pacing the length of her sparsely furnished stone sitting room.

A fireplace crackled in the hearth She stormed past the single couch and low table. The only occupants to witness her fuming rage were the various potted plants and flowers scattered around. Little globs of floating sunlight circled each one, providing the necessary light for them to grow in the underground room.

Neri ran her hands through her russet-brown hair and over her horns. She stomped again, her leathery green wings flaring in her frustration as she neared the door that led to her personal chambers. Neri had turned around for another pass across the room when she paused. The fire in the fireplace moved like a drunken dancer. She gritted her teeth. She didn't need to burn the room again, not after she had finally replaced all the plants she had lost last time.

Taking a deep breath to try to center herself, she waited a couple of seconds.

Nope. Wasn't working.

With the burning urge to do something, *break* something, Neri stalked over to the rack of weapons she kept near the door that led to her bedroom. Swords, axes, a spear that was half charred, and—her personal favorite—a bardiche lay against the wood. Neri grabbed one of the axes and stalked towards the little table. It was the easiest thing to replace in the room.

She stopped in front of the table and firmly planted her feet. She adjusted her grip on the shaft and swung up.

A knock echoed through the room.

Neri froze.

Another knock came from the door leading outside.

"WHAT!" she shouted at the door.

The metal hinges creaked, and a familiar head of messy brown hair popped into view. Neri's father, Duroka, took in the axe she held above her head and the fire that still writhed in the fireplace. His hazel eyes met her bright yellow ones, and he sighed as he stepped into the room.

"Your mother sent another letter, didn't she?" he said as he closed the door behind him. When Neri said nothing, he walked over and gently took the weapon from her. Neri's arms fell limp at her sides as Duroka examined the axe in his hands. He gave a thoughtful hum and then placed it back on the rack with the other weapons.

Since he stood just over six feet tall, Neri had to look up to make eye contact, even though she wasn't that short herself. As he appeared now, Duroka could easily pass for a human, even though that couldn't be further from the truth. Her father was a dragon. And he served as a scout for the Elderwyrm, the dragon strongest in both physical and magical abilities, who presided over their territory. Neri's entire world was ruled by dragons, and she got off rather lucky being a half-dragon-half-human, known as a drakin. Humans were at the bottom of the food chain.

All dragons could take on a human form, but there were a few features that made them stand out. The most noticeable was their height. Their human bodies reflected how big they were in their original form. The largest dragon could easily be ten feet tall, while the smaller ones, like her father, could maybe pass for a tall human. Dragons also tended to retain some features from their draconic form: an unusual hair shade, or eyes that were too vibrant. Her father's tell was the yellow—his natural eye color—that mixed with the brown of his hazel eyes.

"You need to stop letting her get to you like this," Duroka said.

Neri bared her fangs and gave a halfhearted snarl. "She abandons us and then has the *gall* to ask for better accommodations."

"Ah. She must be having trouble getting something from her new—"

"Boy toy."

"I was going to say something else, but sure. That works too." Duroka sighed and looked at the fire. "Do you know why she and I got together?"

"Because humans that help to produce half-breeds like me get better living conditions than those outside the mountain."

"Yes. And I was picked because I was at the bottom of the pecking order. Our relationship was chosen for both of us. After you were born, she found a way to move higher up that order. Specifically, to a dragon that could provide her with more. And while I'm not happy about being left like that, she gave me something incredibly more important. You."

Neri made a gagging motion. "Ugh. No. Stop with that sappy stuff."

The corners of Duroka's lips twitched upwards. "What? Don't like it when your old man tells you how much he loves you?"

Neri grimaced and stuck her tongue out at her father. It was her only defense. In truth, it warmed her heart to hear him being so open with his affections, but she would die before she admitted it.

"You really are the strangest dragon I've met," she said in an attempt to change the subject.

"I'll take that as a compliment."

The room settled into a peaceful quiet as the two regarded each other. The fire dimmed down and the temperature started to cool as a result.

Another knock came from her door.

"What is it now?" Neri sighed as she walked over to the door and threw it open. A slightly startled drakin stood on the other side, with grey wings and ram horns that curled around his head. Neri recognized him from around the mountain, but for the life of her, she couldn't remember his name.

He quickly regained his composure and gave an apologetic smile.

"I've been sent to inform you that your presence has been requested in the main chambers."

Neri's stomach dropped. The main chambers were where the Elderwyrm resided when he wasn't curled up among his hoard.

Duroka, who had been standing a respectful distance away, stepped forward. The drakin's green eyes widened and he immediately dropped into a bow.

"Honored Drake."

Duroka waved his hand dismissively at the title. "What is this about the main chambers?"

The drakin didn't move from his position.

"Ryoka has been summoned to the main chambers. And I believe you have been too, sir."

Neri grimaced at her draconic name. It wasn't that she hated it, but she preferred the name her human aunt had given her.

"Thank you. Dismissed," Duroka said, and the drakin bowed deeper and scrambled to leave.

Neri glanced over her shoulder and up at her father. She quickly recognized the mask that moved into place across his features.

"We should get going before the Great One grows impatient," he grunted. Neri nodded and stepped outside, pulling a key from her pocket to lock the door, Duroka a step behind her.

While the stone hallway was large enough for even the bigger dragons to easily walk through, Neri noticed Duroka chose to stay in his human form as they began down the large, echo-prone tunnel. One of the downsides to living in a mountain was that a constant chill permeated the air, which was compounded by the magic of the Elderwyrm. It made Neri thankful that she had a connection with fire that allowed her to warm herself up slightly.

As they left the section where the drakins lived and moved deeper into the mountain, Duroka changed back into his original form. One second, Neri walked beside her father, and the next she found herself standing beside a large green-scaled leg. She paused and looked up at Duroka, who shook himself out for a second after the transformation. He stood on four legs and had a pair of wings at his back. Two horns adorned his head.

As small as he was, if Neri stood on her tippy-toes, she could brush her fingers across the scales on his underbelly, the most vulnerable place on a dragon. As if sensing her thoughts, Duroka looked down at her with his large, yellow reptilian eyes.

"What? Something on my scales?"

"No. You look fine. I was just thinking about something."

A rumble emanated from Duroka, which Neri felt in her bones, as he looked down the tunnel. He snorted before he continued, claws clicking on the stone, and Neri had to jog to keep up. Together they wove their way through the stone tunnels, passing other drakins and dragons.

Eventually, they arrived at the entrance to the main chambers. It was an enormous hole in the stone wall leading to a cavern that had been carved out by tooth and claw. The chill increased the closer they got, and their breath started to cloud in front of them. Once they stepped inside it became absolutely frigid. A thin layer of frost coated the walls and parts of the floor. Large icicles grew from the ceiling, their bases shrouded in darkness—the light didn't reach that high. From the floor rose blocks of ice. At the back of the cavern was a deep shadowy hallway.

Two other occupants stood in the cavern. Another dragon, a wyvern, that had warm brown scales with a smattering of dull green mixed in. She turned and glared at them with piercing red eyes. A healthy distance away stood a drakin with his arms crossed. He appeared to be in his early thirties, with a head of dirty blonde hair, short horns, and black wings that had a purple iridescent sheen. Neri recognized him as Emual.

She jogged over to him while Duroka walked over to the other dragon. Emual briefly glanced at her as she stopped beside him. She gave a small smile in greeting. He looked away. Neri frowned at the cold shoulder, but quickly brushed it off as the ground shook, and a rumbling growl that sounded like ice grating against ice boomed from the shadowy hallway.

The Elderwyrm was coming. ,

With the proper protocol drilled into them since birth, Neri and Emual dropped to their knees and bowed low, their foreheads pressed against the cold stone beneath them, their wings tucked in tight. Neri felt his presence before he entered the cavern. The weight and power the Elderwyrm carried was almost suffocating. Despite this, curiosity gnawed at Neri, as she had never actually seen the Elderwyrm before. Not fully, at least.

Protocol and curiosity warred within her. Curiosity won, as it usually did.

She shifted her head enough to look up and see the colossal loong as he entered the cavern.

The Elderwyrm's claws were as long as she was tall. Shimmering white scales ran along his serpentine body, light grey scales protecting his underbelly. An icy blue mane of fur traveled from his head to the feather-like tuff on the tip of his tail. And like other loongs, he sported two very long whiskers and a pair of deer-like antlers. The tip of the antlers disappeared into the shadows above them. He huffed a breath, causing the air in the room to whip past Neri and dust her hair with a fine layer of frost.

The Elderwyrm stood there for a couple of moments and stared at them individually. Neri couldn't see what the other dragons were doing, but she could feel the tension radiating from Emual.

Eventually, the Elderwyrm's voice rumbled through the room like the sound of ice cracking atop a frozen lake. "I have a mission for the four of you. What I am about to say will not leave this room." A frustrated growl reverberated through the cavern. "Two days ago, a handful of humans stole something from my hoard."

The absurdity of the statement caused Neri to pause. No one, especially a human, would be dumb enough to sneak into an

Elderwyrm's hoard and steal one of their treasures. Dragons were incredibly territorial and possessive of their valuables. Many would die to protect their hoards, and stealing was the quickest way to reach the top of a dragon's kill list. These humans were either very desperate or incredibly stupid.

"They were human mages from Kazmandis," the Elderwyrm continued. Well, that explained how they were able to get in and out of the mountain. The kingdom of Kazmandis was the largest settlement of humans that Neri knew of—a settlement only made possible because of the mages that defended its borders, wielding the uncommon, possibly rare ability that some humans were born with.

"We killed two while the rest escaped. Their tracks head west, where I believe that they will go to one of the two villages along the Bonepeak Mountains before crossing the border. I have already sent a group to one of these villages. You four will go to the other one. You were chosen because of your ability to blend in with humans."

The Elderwyrm paused and swept his gaze over them again.

"The object is magical. Go now. Prepare." With an icy stare, he growled, "I do not need to remind you what happens if you allow them to cross those mountains with my treasure."

After she had packed a knapsack and collected her bardiche, Neri made her way through the halls of the mountain to the western entrance. Gusts of wind and the sounds of birds chirping greeted her when she stepped out of the corridor and into the large stone cave. An opening across from her showed clear blue skies and gentle rays of sunshine, silhouetting Emual.

Something small and round sailed through the air before a javelin struck it. Emual flicked his wrist and the javelin disappeared from the air, then reappeared in his hand. He pulled a ball of twine off the metal tip, tossed it into the air, and smacked it with his wing, sending it flying across the room again. He pulled his arm back, aimed, and threw the javelin.

Emual hit the twine ball twice more in the time it took Neri to meander closer. He was about to toss it again when she gave an impressed whistle.

Emual jumped and looked in her direction, scowling. "Hefrim's bane. You're quiet," he muttered.

Neri smiled innocently. Emual was turning to practice again when the wyvern walked in. She sauntered over to the cave entrance, but not before glaring at Neri and Emual. Neri's wings twitched and she fought back a defensive snarl. Now that the wyvern was closer, Neri could see where a frill was pulled in close along her slender neck, rippling when the wyvern caught Neri watching. She quickly averted her eyes.

The tension lessened when Duroka padded into the room, carrying a wicker basket in his teeth. It was large enough for a handful of people to stand in it. Neri scowled at the reminder that she would not be flying on this trip. Drakins were grounded—unable to fly. A custom that came about after the drakin rebellion over six hundred years ago.

Full-blooded dragons now believed it was taboo and an insult to their pride for a drakin to retain their ability of flight. So, in the early years of their lives, drakins had a tendon severed in their wings that prevented them from producing a powerful enough downstroke to get airborne. They kept most of the mobility in their wings, but couldn't fly. Every single drakin carried the scars from the incision, even Neri.

17

But Neri's scars were a lie that hid her father's treason.

Duroka placed the basket down near the opening of the cave. "Alright, you two get in and we can be off. It'll most likely be a full day of flying."

Without a word, Emual climbed in, javelin and bag in hand. Neri threw her knapsack into the basket and hopped in with her bardiche.

The wyvern turned around with a snarl aimed at Duroka. "I will not be carrying that thing, runt."

Duroka bristled at the name. "Somani, you are larger than I am. If I were to carry it, we would be slowed down."

"I will not be lowered to a pack animal," she snorted.

"Then you can explain to the Great One why we got to the village late and the mages were allowed to cross the mountains."

Neri and Emual watched the exchange quietly. Eventually, Somani hissed her displeasure, walked over to the basket, and grabbed it with one large claw. Neri had a second to brace herself for the drop before it hit. Her stomach did a familiar flip before Somani pulled up and leveled off.

Before long, the two dragons were soaring through the air. Emual sat down and got comfortable for the long trip. Neri remained standing, the wind buffeting her hair and wings. She loved the feeling of the wind on her face. It was a freeing sensation that she didn't get to experience often, especially under the mountain.

The trip went smoothly. The sun was beginning to set when Somani set them down near the forest at the bottom of the Bonepeak Mountains, which were visible in the distance. Even from here, Neri could see the towering pillars of rock and the snow that dusted the tips of the mountain range. In the morning, they would most likely be able to see the fragments of bones sticking out of the stone. The last resting place of one of the first Elderwyrms.

Camp was made and the night passed without incident. In the morning, everyone prepared to walk the rest of the way to the village. Neri focused her magic on herself and used the other ability she had inherited from Duroka. Her wings, horns, and fangs disappeared, and without looking, she knew that her normally yellow eyes had changed to a muddy brown. A few feet away, Emual did the same. Neri also wrapped an enchanted green ribbon around her bardiche. Once the knot was tied, the illusion spell activated, and the blade of the weapon vanished. Emual wrapped his javelin in sheepskin so that it wouldn't be apparent what he carried. In dragon territories, humans weren't allowed to have weapons, and they needed to pass as humans.

Duroka and Somani took on their human forms. Duroka smiled at Neri as he rolled his shoulders after the transformation. Somani flexed her hands and scowled. Her human form stood at six and a half feet with long brown hair that flowed to her hips. When she looked up, there was a thin ring of red around the pupils of her gray eyes.

"Let's get this over with," she growled, and began the walk to the village.

It appeared like every other village in the Elderwyrm's territory that Neri had seen before. Low buildings and wide dirt streets built to allow dragons to walk through unhindered. They split up to cover more ground. Emual and Somani each went their separate ways, while Duroka and Neri wandered the streets together.

Duroka talked happily about the small things he had learned during his time as a scout, which had him out in villages like this one on several occasions. Neri rarely left the mountain and surrounding area where she had been born. Whenever she did, it was because Duroka had snuck her out for their secret lessons.

They meandered through the village while the residents went about their day as if dragons weren't among them. Kids ran in packs through the streets. Adults exchanged goods or talked. And somewhere in the distance, a flute played a jaunty tune. Surprisingly, a tavern and a couple of shops were scattered throughout the village. Neri stopped in front of one of said shops and looked at the miscellaneous goods displayed behind the dirty glass. A slightly worn-looking blue gown caught her attention.

Duroka took a few steps before he noticed Neri had stopped. He doubled back and peered at the items with her.

"We're far enough away from the mountain that fewer dragons come here. The people this close to the border tend to have more, or can be more open with what they have," he said, and then paused. "Why don't you take a look inside for a few minutes? Ask the merchant if they have anything from the mountain. If you find something you like, get it, but don't take too long. I'll keep looking around outside and cover for both of us."

Duroka grabbed her hand and placed something that clinked in it. Neri looked down at the coins in her palm in shock. Her father merely smiled and quickly walked away, leaving Neri to do whatever she wanted.

Neri stood there for a couple of minutes before she felt someone come to a stop beside her. A young woman, around her own age, with bronze skin and long black hair stood with her arms crossed. A person with her appearance wasn't a common sight this far north. Neri couldn't help but wonder if she was, or had family, from the east, where merchants were rarely allowed to journey between Elderwyrm territories. The woman wore plain brown trousers, a beige long-sleeved shirt, and a deep blue vest. A pouch hung from a belt around her waist.

"Got an interesting variety," she hummed to herself. A pause. She looked over at Neri with a smile. "Do I have to stake my claim on something now, or are you just looking?"

"Pardon?"

"You were just eyeing that blue dress in the window. Do I have to fight you over it or not?"

Neri opened her mouth to argue back, but stopped. She had indeed been looking at the dress. In all her years, she had never owned a dress, and a chance like this made her want to go in and buy it on impulse.

Drakins were soldiers, tools for the dragons, so they didn't have opportunities to own fancy clothing or anything special that didn't further their usefulness. Neri got away with her plants, but that was as far as she had been able to push the rules. Owning a dress that was hers alone was a dream she had held for nearly a decade now.

She must have made a face, because the young woman beside her threaded her arm through Neri's and whispered conspiratorially, "I can tell you want something nice. Follow me. I got you covered."

Neri didn't have time to argue before the young woman yanked her into the store. A bell attached to the door jingled as they entered.

"I'm Adara, by the way," she said over her shoulder as she pulled Neri through the shelves and towards the counter in the back.

"Neri. What are you doing?"

"Helping you find something nice. Trust me."

"I just met you."

"Shhhh. Trust me. I know where the good merchandise is."

"Is that anything to do with the mountain? My father told me to ask about something from the mountain."

Adara smiled and pulled her to a stop before the counter, where a balding man with a thick beard looked up with a raised brow. Adara sidled up to the counter, slid something across the wood, and whispered to the man. Neri looked over Adara's shoulder to see what she had handed him, but the merchant quickly whisked the item off the counter and nodded. He smiled pleasantly at Adara and Neri and gestured for them to follow him.

Adara bounded forward while Neri followed cautiously behind them. They came to a small back room littered with boxes. Something smelled different here, but Neri couldn't put her finger on it. The man pushed aside a few boxes, revealing a trapdoor in the floor.

"This is definitely not suspicious at all," Neri muttered.

Adara looked over her shoulder. "First time buying smuggled goods?"

"Yeah."

"Well, there's a first time for everything," Adara said as the man pulled up the door. A narrow wooden ladder went about five feet down into a dimly lit room. Neri sniffed again; the strange smell seemed stronger now.

"You can leave your stuff up here. No one will touch it," the man said, gesturing toward a corner hidden from the front by boxes. "Your walking stick would be troublesome to get down the ladder."

Neri's grip on her bardiche tightened momentarily before she relented. She gingerly placed it against a box, the blade turned away so that someone wouldn't get hurt if they brushed against it, but she kept her knapsack on.

Adara slid down the ladder first. Neri followed, then the merchant came down and closed the trapdoor behind him. Neri blinked in the dim light. Shelves lined the walls of the smaller room and open boxes ran down the middle. Bottles, clothes, books, and even a few old weapons were scattered around. Neri cautiously walked around while Adara glided from one shelf to another. While Neri kept one eye on the two humans, she allowed herself to relax some. On the off chance that one of them pulled out a weapon or jumped her, she could easily throw them across the room or summon fire.

As Adara chatted away with the merchant, Neri picked up a bottle. A single piece of parchment was attached to its neck by a thin line of string. Neri flipped the label over and read the handwritten words. It was a potent medicine made from a flower only found in Kazmandis, nearly impossible to find closer to the mountain.

"I knew goods were smuggled across the border, but I never realized how much managed to get across," Neri said as she put the medicine back.

"It's not easy or without risk, but it does help that most dragons think so little of us that they don't anticipate how creative we can get," the merchant responded, walking to the back of the room.

Adara gasped behind her. "Neri, this would look great on you!" she exclaimed. Neri turned around to see her holding up a simple green dress. Sheepishly, she walked over and ran her hand across the cotton material. It looked brand new and pretty.

Adara held it up to her and squinted. "I think it goes well with your hair and eyes. I daresay that green really is your color."

Neri gave a small smile. "You're not wrong."

The dress was nice. Neri put her hand in her pocket and palmed the coins her father had given her. She decided she would buy it if she had enough money.

Adara tilted her head to the side as she watched Neri look over the dress. "You don't get out and shop much, do you?"

"No. I've never even owned a dress."

"What? Your mother never made you one?"

Neri scowled at the mention of her mother.

Adara's smile faltered and a knowing look swept over her face. She sighed. "Not on good terms with your mother either, huh?" she asked as she leaned against a box and gently laid the dress out on it.

Neri shook her head and snorted. "That's putting it mildly. Sounds like you're in a similar situation."

"My parents want my twin brother and me to be like our grand-parents. They're highly respected in the community, so there's al-ready pressure to live up to the family name." Adara ran her hand absentmindedly across the dress. "Mom puts a lot of expectations on me. Dad does the same with my brother. Let's just say that he and I fled from home to write our own futures."

"Doing what?"

"Coming here." Adara paused and thought for a second. "Our mentor had an errand to run, so we came with him to help. I may have slipped away for a little shopping trip, though."

"Little?"

Adara smirked. "Hey, it's never fun to shop by yourself. I'd say the distraction was worth it. I didn't think I would be there for someone's first dress."

"Thanks," Neri chuckled. "I should be getting back to my fa-ther, though. I've been away a while. Excuse me, sir, how much is this dress?"

Neri walked out of the store with a smile on her face, bardiche in hand and her new dress carefully wrapped and placed in her knapsack. Adara, right behind her, twirled happily and wrapped her new dark blue scarf around her neck. They had taken a few steps forward, laughing, when the sound of a dog barking brought them to a halt.

A large, fuzzy black dog skidded to a stop in front of Adara. He wagged his tail, which curled up and over his body, and nuzzled her hand. Adara chuckled and scratched his ears.

"Hey, Finnik. If you're here, that means…"

"Adara!" shouted a young man, the spitting image of Adara, as he ran up to them. He gave Neri a brief smile in greeting, then glared at Adara. "Where have you been? I've been looking everywhere for you. Tallak is almost done finalizing a deal for transportation." He gestured wildly; the bone beads of a strange bracelet clinked with his movement.

"Cerdic, I've—"

"I'm sure your excuse is a good one, Miss Dalgaard," said a man as he approached. He had short blonde hair, a trimmed beard, and a bag slung over one shoulder. He walked with an air of authority and a look that suggested he wouldn't take no for an answer. Neri began to feel as if she were intruding.

"I… I've… Sorry, sir," Adara muttered, looking everywhere but at him.

Neri quickly scanned the area and saw Duroka not far away, talking with a man in the doorway of a building. She turned to Adara. "I should probably get going. Thank you for your time. I had fun."

As she turned to leave, a gentle breeze picked up. A crisp, woody scent hit Neri's nose and she paused. The dog perked up and sniffed the air. He turned to Neri and stared at her with unusually intelligent golden eyes.

What dog had gold eyes?

His lips curled back, baring his fangs. His hackles rose. A low rumbling growl sounded. The dog positioned himself between the humans and Neri. Adara looked down, confused, and Tallak's brow furrowed.

"Wait a minute. That's…" Cerdic began, but was interrupted as a hand landed on Neri's shoulder.

Neri nearly transformed from the fright, but was quickly reassured when a familiar scent washed over her. Duroka gave her shoulder a gentle squeeze.

"Is everything alright?" he asked.

The dog barked twice and then retreated to Cerdic's side with a growl. The three humans tensed and eyed each other.

"We're good. Thanks," Tallak said, readjusting his grip on his bag. Duroka's eyes narrowed, and he subtly sniffed the air. A low rumble vibrated from his chest, and he slowly pulled Neri behind him.

"You have something that doesn't belong to you," Duroka said quietly.

"Oh?" Tallak said. He stepped in front of Adara and Cerdic. Adara shot Neri a concerned look and slowly reached toward the pouch around her waist.

"I can smell it in the bag. Hand it over and we don't have to fight."

"Afraid I can't do that," Tallak said, and slipped the bag to Adara.

Neri looked around, tightening her grip on her weapon. She was conflicted. She didn't want to fight them, but she would if she had to. She shifted the knapsack off her shoulder and dropped it to the ground behind her. If she shifted, the straps would get caught on her wings.

The two groups stood there, staring at each other.

Tallak's hand shot out. A wave of fire spiraled from his palm and engulfed Neri and Duroka. Neri blinked at the sudden flare of light. The warmth of the fire washed over her, embracing her with its familiarity.

As quickly as they started, the flames vanished. Someone on the street screamed.

"Seriously?" Neri sighed and glanced down at the small burns scattered across her clothes.

"Shit," Cerdic muttered.

"Last chance," Duroka growled, equally unhurt by the attack.

Tallak gritted his teeth and drew the handle of a sword from his pocket. "Kids," he said. "RUN!"

Tallak charged Duroka, a blade of ice erupting from the hilt in his hands. Duroka grunted as he dodged out of the way. People on the street scattered in any direction that led away from Neri and the others. Shouts filled the air, quickly making it hard to hear.

"Finnik, find us a path out of here!" Cerdic called. The dog's form shifted and compacted in on itself until a raven with golden eyes launched into the air. He cawed and was gone.

Adara darted down the road with Cerdic on her heels. Neri ripped the ribbon off her bardiche, the blade materializing back into view, and ran after them. Clearly, the mages had never fought a drakin before, and didn't realize how fast they were compared to humans.

The thrill of the chase and the fight made her blood sing. The distance between them quickly vanished until Neri bounded around and came to a stop in front of the group, bardiche pointed at their chests. She couldn't let them leave the village.

The twins skidded to a stop before her. Adara pulled a wand out of her pouch and pointed it at Neri. The two women paused, but Cerdic didn't hesitate.

"If fire won't work…" he said under his breath, and smacked his hand down on the dirt road.

The bone bracelet around his wrist glowed and a pulse of energy traveled through the ground. Neri stumbled as the earth shook and heaved, a pile of rock and dirt forming where Cerdic's hand had hit. The pile grew until it was as tall as the nearest building, and a stout humanoid form took shape. Neri reverted to her draconic form as the earth elemental straightened itself and turned towards her. She flared her wings and snarled out a challenge.

Neri jumped out of the way as a stone fist slammed into the ground. She swung her bardiche into the elemental, cutting deeply into its arm. The elemental made no noise as it swatted at her with its other hand. Neri pulled the blade free and ducked under the attack.

They continued their little dance until a familiar javelin impaled the earth elemental's chest. Emual ran by her, wings out and fangs bared. He used the javelin to vault himself up and on top of the construct, then jumped onto a nearby roof. With a flick of his wrist, the javelin disappeared and then reappeared in his right hand.

Movement caught Neri's eye. Adara and Cerdic sprinted past her and continued down the road. Emual's head whipped in their direction.

"They have the Elderwyrm's treasure!" Neri yelled as she dodged another blow from the elemental. Emual nodded and rushed after them along the rooftops.

A roar echoed through the village, followed by people screaming and running back in her direction. In the distance, Somani reared her head above the buildings and let loose another roar, the frill around her neck flaring out.

Blocking out the sound, Neri darted forward, swung, and hit the elemental's leg. The construct fell silently to one knee. She tightened her grip and went for the head, only for the thing to vanish suddenly.

Neri pulled her swing short and looked around nervously. Something that big couldn't have just disappeared like that. She sniffed the air; even the scent of freshly dug earth was gone. Neri slowly backed up, her head on a swivel.

Movement in the air. Neri turned. There was nothing—

Something hard slammed into her and sent her flying into a nearby house. The impact on the stone wall knocked the breath out of her and she landed on the ground with a grunt. It was moments like this that she was grateful to be part dragon. Her sturdier bones prevented anything from breaking, particularly her wings.

With a groan, Neri pulled herself up to a kneeling position and looked around. Her bardiche lay a few feet away. She shook her head to clear her vision and started to reach for it when a shadow loomed over her.

Her heart skipped a beat as the earth elemental towered above, standing between her and her weapon. Despite her protesting body, Neri dove away from the elemental and her bardiche. In the time it took for the thing to turn around, she jumped to her feet. The elemental reared back for a swing, but there was no time to dodge. She reached out and caught the punch with both hands. Her skull rattled with the impact. The elemental pulled back its other arm. Neri moved one hand to catch the swing.

They stood locked together, each pushing to see if the other would give. Neri hissed through her teeth, her muscles burning as she held back the immense strength of the earth elemental. It leaned into her, and Neri's feet slid back a fraction on the dirt path. She looked around for a solution. Heating the rock would take too long—she had to think of something else.

The air rippled as something moved beside her. Neri's eyes narrowed. It was the same sign that gave away her brother whenever he tried to sneak up on her back home.

She had to get away from the elemental. Neri tucked in her wings and hands, lunged forward, and rolled between the construct's legs. The resistance gone, the elemental tumbled forward and fell with a loud *thud* to the ground. In one motion, Neri jumped up from the roll and swept her hand out. A line of fire shot forth and arced in the air before her. A couple of yelps sounded as the illusion faded and Cerdic and Adara, bag in hand, dove to the ground to avoid the fire.

Neri rushed forward, but Cerdic was faster. His hand with the bracelet shot out and Neri ran face-first into a glowing protective ward that encircled the twins. Neri barked a curse; her hand flew to her nose. Cerdic helped Adara to her feet, hand still held out, a bead of sweat trickling down his temple. He was breathing heavily, and Neri wasn't sure if it was from the fight or the energy required to maintain the ward.

The siblings backed up until they were in an alley. Adara looked back, her shoulders slumping as she realized their mistake. The alley was a dead end. She turned back around and pointed her wand at Neri, fear and betrayal written on her face.

30

Neri walked up to the ward and placed both hands on the magical barrier. "I'll admit you had me fooled for a little while there, masking your scent and sound too," she said. "Unfortunately for you, my brother also deals with illusions."

"Neri, just let us go," Adara pleaded.

"I can't do that. Not with the Elderwyrm's treasure."

"Please."

Neri's wings flared and she slammed her fist against the barrier. "I don't want to fight you!"

"Then why do you fight?" Adara shouted back.

"Because now that we know you have it, if we don't return with that"—Neri jabbed a finger at the bag—"he will kill us."

"We can't give it up. What we might learn about the Elderwyrm's magic could save our people."

"Adara…" Cerdic hissed through gritted teeth. His hand had started to shake.

Neri opened her mouth to respond, but stopped as Emual rounded the corner, javelin in hand, and slid to a stop next to her. He scowled at Adara and Cerdic. It seemed he had figured out that he'd been chasing after illusions.

Adara's eyes darted from Emual to Neri. The twins exchanged glances. Cerdic nodded. A steely determination settled over Adara's features and she hid the bag behind her.

For the sake of herself and Duroka, Neri would do what it took to get the treasure back. Even if it made her heart ache.

"Help me break the barrier," she muttered to Emual.

The drakin grunted his acknowledgment, took a few steps away, and lifted up his javelin. Neri pulled her hands back a fraction and let a flame bloom from her palm. The fire quickly spread from her hand and wrapped around the magical ward. Emual pulled his arm back and chucked his weapon at the barrier. It hit with a loud *clang.* Neri's fire grew hotter, and a strained grunt sounded from inside.

A shadow suddenly loomed over the alley. Neri and Emual spun around, expecting to see the earth elemental, but they found themselves facing something even more dangerous.

Somani towered over the buildings. Her crimson eyes narrowed as she took in the scene. The humans were trapped with nowhere to go besides up, and the only things that stood between her and the mages were Neri and Emual. Neri grimaced. They just had to get stuck with a dragon that hated drakins.

Somani's frill fanned out around her head, displaying reds and yellows, and she hissed at them, a gleeful look to her sneer. She took in a deep breath and opened her maw wide.

Emual flinched and turned to bolt. Neri took a shaky step back. They couldn't outrun Somani's acid breath. Wedged between the wyvern and the mages in the barrier, their only option was up. An option that was supposed to be impossible for drakins. All drakins but Neri.

As Somani unleashed a torrent of acid, Neri leaped into the air. A roar of pain echoed from Emual. The sound quickly shifted to a wet gurgle before falling silent. Neri's gut twisted with shame that she hadn't reached out to try to grab him. She beat her wings until she was high enough, landed on a nearby roof, and spun around.

The ward was gone. Adara and Cerdic huddled together within a ring of smoking stone and brick. They were unscathed aside from a few patches where the acid had splattered when the magic barrier had broken. Further down the alley lay half a torso that Neri refused to look at too long. At the very end stood Somani, her jaw slightly ajar as she stared at Neri.

Somani quickly shook herself back to reality and growled, her voice dripping with venom, "*You...*"

Neri glanced at the mages, who were staring open-mouthed, and then back at Somani. She positioned herself to face the wyvern, looked her in the eyes, and bared her fangs in a snarl. Flames started to form around her hands.

The mages were momentarily forgotten as Somani stalked toward Neri.

"You will die for this transgression, and then I will rip out the throat of your treasonous fa—"

A roar of feral fury shook the village before a smaller green shape barreled into Somani. Both of them crashed into a nearby building in a shower of wooden splinters and stone shards. Duroka jumped onto Somani's back and sank his teeth into the scales of her neck. Somani howled and thrashed around, reducing another house to rubble in seconds. The wyvern reared up, twisted her body, and slammed down into the ground, back first. Duroka grunted in pain and lost his grip on Somani.

The two dragons scrambled to their feet, hissing and spitting at each other. Somani lunged at the smaller dragon. Duroka ducked under her and leaped into the air, Somani not far behind him. The two of them twisted together in the air, fire and acid flying.

Neri's stomach lurched. She took a hesitant step forward. While she was no match for a full-grown dragon, she couldn't just leave her father to fend for himself. Because of his size, he was at a significant disadvantage when fighting other dragons. She watched helplessly as he and Somani crashed into the woods near the village. Hard enough that she felt the ground shake slightly. While it would have hurt, the fall wouldn't have killed either of them, which meant her father would still be out there fighting for his life—and hers.

The screeching of the two fighting dragons echoed in the distance. Neri wanted to help, but she also couldn't just leave the mages with the Elderwyrm's treasure. She looked between the mages and the woods. Adara stopped checking on Cerdic and glanced up at her. Neri bit her lip as she thought, gazing towards the woods again.

A roar of defiance reached her ears. Duroka.

Neri kicked the roof in frustration, a puff of smoke escaping from between her gritted teeth. She jumped off the roof and flew towards where her bardiche lay on the dirt road. She kicked aside some rubble and picked it up. Gripping the familiar wooden shaft, Neri leaped into the air, banking towards the woods.

Adara carefully picked her way out of the alley, Cerdic not far behind her. The surrounding area looked as if a tornado had rolled through. At the sound of rocks moving, she jumped and spun around, wand and magic ready.

Tallak rounded a large pile of rubble, his shoulders slumping in relief at the sight of them. Apart from a nasty cut above his eye, blood seeping from the wound, and some burned patches on his clothes, he didn't appear seriously injured.

"Are you two alright?" he asked as he approached.

"We're fine. What about you?" Adara said.

"I'll live."

"What just happened?" Cerdic gestured to where the dragons had destroyed a handful of buildings.

"Dragon politics, I would assume, but I'm not about to question a gift from the heavens. Where's Finnik?"

As if hearing his name, Finnik flew down and landed on Cerdic's outstretched arm. The púca stared at each of them quizzically with a tilt of his head.

"Great. Now that we're all here, let's leave quickly before the dragons settle their differences." Tallak turned and started to walk towards the Bonepeak Mountains.

Cerdic moved to follow, but Adara hesitated. She looked over her shoulder at the woods, where she could still hear the blood-chilling roars of the dragons.

"Wait!" she called out.

Tallak and Cerdic paused.

"The Headmaster is looking for possible allies, right? Well, we might have just found two," Adara said. "The half-dragon and the green one seem different. We attacked them first and they still gave us a chance for a peaceful solution. How many dragons do you know that would do that for humans? If we leave now, we might be dooming powerful allies."

Tallak stared at the woods, deep in thought.

Neri wove through the trees, heading in the direction of her father and Somani. Years of secret flying lessons from Duroka allowed her to maneuver around the branches and trunks with ease. On top of the booming roars, she could hear her heart hammering in her head. Her only thought was to get to her father in time.

The trunk of a tree suddenly splintered and went flying in her direction. Neri had to tuck in her wings and dive to avoid it. Flapping wildly to steady herself, she looked up at the scene before her.

Duroka was running between trees to avoid Somani's tail as it crashed into another trunk and destroyed it in a shower of splinters. Somani roared, frill flaring, then sprayed the area with more acid. The ground was already a turned-up, frothy mush from her previous attacks.

Duroka darted out, leaped over the acidic ground, and collided with Somani. He managed to get a few deep slashes in her sides with his claws before she bucked and sent him crashing into more trees, the wood snapping under his weight. Duroka scrambled to his feet, swayed for a second, and snarled. There was a wild look in his yellow eyes that Neri wasn't familiar with, and it unnerved her. She flew over and landed on a thick tree branch to wait for an opening.

It didn't take long. As Neri stood perched on the branch, Somani reared up and unfurled her wings to their full length. A show of dominance among dragons. Neri kicked off of the branch and dove straight for the wyvern, bardiche held out in front of her.

Somani was too distracted by Duroka to notice until it was too late. Neri went straight for the wyvern's wing, shoving the point of her blade into the unprotected membrane and swinging down with all her might. Somani's scream of pain made Neri's ears ring as she cut the membrane from the bone to the bottom of the wing. Somani jerked away, and Neri used that moment to dart off to another tree.

"Who's grounded now, you overgrown skink?" she shouted.

Somani's savage red eyes locked on Neri and widened as the realization hit. A small tear or hole in a dragon's wing wouldn't be a problem, but a large injury could keep them from flight. Neri smirked, flipped the giant lizard off, and swooped to a nearby tree, just before acid hit where she had been standing.

Neri flew from one tree to another while Somani spat acid her way, all the while keeping Duroka at bay with her tail and teeth. A croak-like caw sounded above them, and Neri peeked around the tree she was hiding behind. A familiar-looking raven circled above Somani and cawed again. Somani paused and looked up—just in time for the raven to dive down at her. He immediately latched onto her face and started to peck and claw at her eye. Somani screeched and threw her head back, dislodging the raven. He quickly flew off with a croaking laugh, blood dripping from his talons and beak.

Somani, one eye weeping blood, spun around and opened her mouth. Duroka darted out and jumped at her again. She whipped around and spat more acid, only for it to pass harmlessly through him. The image of Duroka shimmered and vanished as the illusion dropped. Somani snorted in frustration, scanning the area.

A short whistle drew Neri's attention to the bottom of the tree she had perched on. On the ground stood Tallak, who looked up and gestured for her to come down. Neri tilted her head to the side. What were they doing here? Why didn't they leave when they had the chance?

She looked over her shoulder at Somani as another illusion charged her. Tallak whistled again and pointed vehemently at the ground. Curiosity, and a smidge of desperation, got the better of Neri, and she dropped down. His hand not far from his sword, the older mage took a cautious step back as she landed and looked her over. Neri held her bardiche in a relaxed manner, hoping he wouldn't see it as a threatening stance.

"Yes?" she asked.

"We're here to help."

"So it would seem."

"Adara wants to help you, and she provided a decent argument, so right now we have a common enemy. I need to get close to that wyvern, but I can't do it on my own while the ground is an acid pit." He paused and gritted his teeth. "For this plan to work, I'm going to need you to fly me to her face."

"You want me to fly you?" Neri asked incredulously. "To her face. Do you have a death wish?"

"We need to stop her from spitting more acid. I can do that, but I need to be close to her mouth."

Neri fiddled with the shaft of her bardiche. Stopping the acid would level the playing field for everyone, and it might give Duroka the opening he needed to take Somani down. She looked at Tallak. While he appeared hesitant to trust her, he had still approached someone he had probably grown up thinking of as an enemy.

Somani roared, and the crackling of fire sounded behind them.

Neri planted the blade of her bardiche into the ground and held out her empty hands. Tallak glanced at them, then down at his sword handle. He tucked it into his belt and grabbed her hands with his callused fingers. Neri tried to give a reassuring smile, crouched, and launched herself in the air.

A grunt of surprise sounded from below as Neri worked to gain altitude. She beat her wings frantically until she cleared the treetops. From this vantage point, Neri could see Duroka stalking among the trees while Somani snapped at illusion after illusion, her growls of frustration ringing in Neri's ears.

Neri banked until she was behind Somani, then waited. When an opening presented itself, she tucked in her wings and dove. Tallak's grip turned painful as the wind whipped by. Somani was too distracted to notice them, and when they were close enough, Neri spread her wings out and allowed the drag to slow them down. When they were over Somani's head, Neri lowered Tallak until his feet almost touched her, and then let him go. She immediately darted underneath Somani and made a beeline to a tree.

The air behind her dropped suddenly. Somani's roar was muffled by the crackling sound of ice growing. Neri reached the tree and spun around. Tallak had straddled Somani's snout. Both hands were wrapped around the sword hilt embedded in a block of ice that had formed around her open mouth. Somani's one remaining eye rolled wildly as choking sounds emanated from her throat. Tallak gritted his teeth as the wyvern started to shake her head.

Duroka rushed out of the woods and knocked her to the ground. Tallak managed to keep his grip on his sword hilt, holding on for dear life as Duroka pinned Somani to the floor. Somani flailed and kicked, but Duroka sidestepped her attempts and lunged at her throat. He bit down, blood spraying and hitting his face.

It took a few moments for Somani's movements to turn sluggish and then stop. Once she remained unmoving, Duroka released his hold on her and shook his head. Then he turned to where Tallak still held on to Somani.

He lowered his head until it was under Tallak. The mage tensed until he realized Duroka was giving him somewhere to jump that wasn't the acid-covered ground. Tallak pulled his sword hilt free and jumped down. Duroka slowly stood up and carefully picked a path through the acid patches until he stood near the trees. He lowered his snout and Tallak slid off onto solid ground.

Neri jumped down from her tree and ran up to them. Duroka's form shifted until he looked human again. He groaned and rolled his shoulders.

"Dad! Are you alright?" Neri quickly looked over him. Numerous cuts and acid burns littered his body. Luckily, nothing looked too severe.

"Nothing a few days of rest won't fix." Duroka sighed and wiped some of the blood off his mouth. He frowned and shook it from his hand. Tallak, who had been standing as if contemplating kissing the ground, turned and stared at them.

"He's your father?" he asked.

Neri gave a small smile. "What? You don't see the family resemblance?"

A familiar voice whooped with glee and Neri turned to see Adara and Cerdic running towards them. Adara grinned and ran up to Neri as if to hug her, but stopped short upon remembering who she was. Her smile faltered.

"Hey," Neri said.

"That was impressive," Adara said.

"I'm told you made a convincing argument to come help us. Thanks."

Adara chuckled. "I can be persuasive when I want to be."

"Who's your new friend?" Duroka asked. Adara glanced at him curiously.

"This is Adara. Adara, this is my father, Duroka." Neri gestured to each of them. Adara gave a polite smile. Duroka wiped the blood off of his hand on his trousers and held it out. It was such a human gesture that the mages looked at him as if he had grown a second head.

Duroka slowly lowered his hand. "Apologies."

"Well, it would appear that we still have a problem before us," Tallak said after a moment.

"Yes. We can't let you leave with the treasure, and you don't want to give it up. But, in all honesty, I'm tired of fighting," Duroka said. The older mage raised an eyebrow. "What did you take? Maybe we can find a solution where we both walk away happy?"

Tallak rubbed his bearded chin as he thought for a minute. Then he turned to Adara and nodded.

Adara stepped forward, bag in hand. She reached in, rummaged around for a second, and pulled out a dark, palm-sized wooden ball that radiated magic, holding it out for Neri and Duroka to see.

Duroka groaned and ran a hand down his face. Neri simply blinked at the ball.

She turned to her father. "He sent us through all that... for *this*?" She gestured at the wooden ball.

"Petty bastard," Duroka sighed.

"What? What is it?" Cerdic asked.

"It's a teething ball for hatchlings. The enchantment allows the wood to regrow."

"A *what*?"

"A chew toy," Neri said.

"You're joking," Adara muttered, looking down at the object in her hand.

"I wish I was."

"Why did you grab this?" Duroka asked.

"We were going for something else, but we were discovered before we could get to it," Tallak explained. "So we grabbed the closest item that had any of the Elderwyrm's magic on it."

"Why were you after the Elderwyrm's magic?" Neri asked.

"War between our people is inevitable. Regular dragons we can plan for, but an Elderwyrm could cause the kind of destruction in days that would take a regular dragon months. If we can study his magic, we can better defend ourselves."

Duroka nodded in understanding. Scratching his head, he sniffed the air and smiled to himself. He turned to Neri with a familiar expression. "What do you smell from it?"

"Seriously?" She sighed. Of course he would choose now to try to give a lesson.

She sniffed the air. Now that it was out of the bag and closer to her, Neri could finally pick up on what had told Duroka that it was in the bag.

"It smells like wood and a freshly frozen lake," she stated finally.

"And what does that mean?"

Neri rolled her eyes. "That he drooled on it a lot when he was a hatchling?"

"Come now, why does your bardiche smell like a forest after a fire?" Neri opened her mouth, but was quickly cut off by Duroka. "And no, it's not because you've burned it a few times."

Neri crossed her arms over her chest and gave a halfhearted growl as she thought, racking her memory for anything that might prove useful. She had to sniff the air again before it hit her.

"Oh!" Her arms dropped to her sides. "Residual magic. He blasted it with his magic enough times that some of it remained on the ball."

"That's my girl." Duroka smiled widely and nudged her arm. Neri's face warmed at the praise, and she huffed a breath and looked away. Duroka turned back to the mages. "In theory, we should be able to cut off a piece that holds a lot of his residual magic and the ball will just regrow that section. You can take the sliver and we'll take the ball."

Tallak eyed him. "Why are you willing to do this for us?"

Duroka bent over and pulled a dagger out of his boot.

"The Elderwyrm doesn't hold my loyalty," he said, holding out his free hand. "May I?"

Adara glanced between Neri and Tallak before slowly placing the ball in Duroka's hand. Between Neri and Duroka, they were quickly able to locate the section that held the most residual magic, and Duroka carved off that slice. He tossed it to the mages while Neri held onto the ball. She watched as the enchantment flared and the wood started to grow and knit itself together until it looked like it had never been carved.

The mages quickly pocketed the sliver of wood. Tallak turned and looked Duroka up and down. He walked up to the dragon and held out his hand. Duroka paused briefly, but returned the handshake.

Adara sidled over to Neri and gave an uncharacteristically shy smile. "Well, it's been fun, but it looks like our little shopping trip is officially over."

"Still calling it 'little,' huh?" Neri scoffed, but smiled. "It has been fun."

"Yeah. And if you ever find yourself in Kazmandis, I'll take you to one of our best stores. They have the finest silks west of the Bonepeak Mountains."

Neri chuckled. "I look forward to it."

Adara smiled and waved as she turned to follow the others, who had started to pick their way through the destruction and towards the mountains. The raven croaked merrily overhead. Neri held the Elderwyrm's ball securely in her hand as she and Duroka watched them walk away.

Her father looked at her back, and then around her. "Where did your bag go?" he asked.

Neri blinked.

"MY DRESS!" she shouted, and bolted back to the village.

II

What If It Kills Your Dragon?

Renée Hill

Burning embers were all that remained of the last oatmeal bar that Amma had been strong enough to make for me. It had slipped through my fingers into the dying fire and now all I could do was stare at the black goo sinking into the ashes. Somehow, after everything else, losing that gift was what broke something inside me.

I curled up on the cold ground—probably too close to the weak flames, but what difference did it make? Two more villagers had died today and the Elders were doing nothing. Maybe it was because we were all so tired.

Clarissima blinked large sleepy eyes at me and blew moist dragon breath on my legs. Was she more lethargic than before the jump? Were her ribs more pronounced under her skin or was that just a trick of the swirls of color? Clarissima had put the idea of time travel into my head--I had not even known it was possible! But she hadn't told me the toll time-jumping would take on her. So was I willing to sacrifice my dragon, my dearest friend, for my village? What if it didn't even help? With dragons so rare these days, how could I even think about endangering Clarissima's life?

When I'd told Amma what I was going to try, she, who barely had strength enough to breathe, had gasped out that traveling back into the past was useless. But nothing the Elders were doing was helping, and I had to do *something*.

Clarissima shifted her massive bulk so that her wing touched my leg. *I can jump again. When do you wish to go, Leena?*

And that was just it. I had no idea how to unravel the curse or when it had been laid upon our ancestors. On my trip I had gone back ten annuals and gathered water, bread, soil, even a musical instrument to strum in case that was the key to breaking the curse. But nothing had helped Amma and now here I was, watching the last gift she had made for me turn to ash.

Rigoret threw himself down by the dying fire, his thick black brows drawn together as they always were lately. He wore a perpetual scowl and was nothing like the musical, artistic brother he had been before Amma got sick. Before she became so tired that she finally let us take over her village tasks. Amma had always been the one who went to the local market each week. Six suns ago, for the first time, Rigoret and I got to go in her place.

We awakened early, as Amma always did: "Get there before only bruised fruit!" I was so excited, my body tingled. I had never been beyond our village borders—only our Amma ever interacted with the strange outside world. And now us!

Rigoret sat beside me on the rickety cart, his neck swiveling this way and that as he took in the sights. The market town looked at least five times the size of our village, with small houses on each side of the road leading in, first spaced apart and then gradually becoming closer and closer until they were crowded together like trees in a forest. I shuddered. Way too close for my liking. But the

WHAT IF IT KILLS YOUR DRAGON?

market! Stalls set up helter skelter in an open field, people selling or bartering all kinds of items. Even as early as we were, all the stalls were open and crowded.

I smiled at Rigoret. This was fun! After we'd paid for the items on our list, we could wander around and delight in the delectable food aromas, fantastically colored flowers and strange, expensive-looking garments.

But I began to feel edgy, my heart rate speeding up as I stared around us. It was only when Rigoret grabbed my arm and squeezed it, motioning for me to follow his gaze, that I realized what was making me anxious. For the first time I saw the real pace of the world.

Children running and skipping.

People walking more than a few paces without having to sit and rest, carrying bags and even moving planks and furniture without the use of mules.

Rigoret and I stared at one another as we sat atop our cart, stunned by the activity and the frenzy with which these people lived. Women were balancing babies and heavy baskets, walking briskly to and fro with enough breath left over to gossip and haggle over prices.

Children were throwing and chasing round things, screaming and yelling at one another, falling over with laughter. It hurt my chest just to watch, and I found myself leaning back against the bench seat on the cart, squeezing my eyes shut against the blinding movement and gasping in air as if I had managed such exertion myself. Rigoret demanded that we drive on to a village like ours, and not a market. But it was the same.

There was something wrong, something dreadfully wrong, with our people.

Our village had stools carefully spaced out, no more than five paces apart, from house to barn, house to house, house to the village meeting place, house to the gardens—the gardens which were replete with so many stools that they resembled mushroom patches. At any moment of the day many villagers would be collapsed on the stools, bent over as they tried to catch their breath and gather strength to take five more steps in their desired direction.

I remembered when I was younger and the stools had been farther apart; some villagers had even had the breath for singing and telling tales. Now conversation consisted of short phrases giving directions or commands. There was little space for praise and none for joy. No women had survived childbirth in the last seven annuals: the mothers had not had the strength to push and the infants had not had the strength to fight.

"When going back?" Rigoret demanded, bringing me out of my gloomy thoughts. He eyed the black goo in the ashes, but said nothing.

"If I go," I responded, "only me." I sucked air into my depleted lungs as I shook my head. Rigoret could not go back in time with me. "Amma!"

"Jolet with Amma." Rigoret stared at me as if he could bend me to his will. "Need me."

I puzzled over that last one. Did he mean Amma needed him? That was what I had said!

He thought I needed him? That must be what he meant. And he was wrong. He needed to stay here and ready Amma for tomorrow's Celebration of the Great Mother because it might be…it

WHAT IF IT KILLS YOUR DRAGON?

might be her last. And our neighbor Jolet was wonderful with Amma, but she could not take our place.

I closed my eyes in frustration. Rigoret never listened. "Go to when?" I asked impatiently. We just didn't have enough information!

"To the old times."

I looked questioningly at him.

"Amma once said Amma-three-times told her the children chased butterflies." Rigoret fell forward, pulling in desperate draws of air after the long statement.

My head snapped up. Yes! I remembered that! Amma used to regale us with stories she had been told as a child about how different things once had been. At the time I had thought butterflies in the past must have sat peacefully on branches, a far cry from the frenetic creatures of today. But what if they'd flown just as fast then? Was it even possible that a child could catch one in their hands? How could anyone move that fast?

I drew a line in the dirt with my finger. The children in the market might be able to move that fast. Had our children been able to chase insects—chase anything!—sometime in the past?

"Clarissima." It had taken me a while to get used to the mind talking that I now took for granted. "Take back to Amma-three-times?"

Yes.

"Strong enough now?"

Yes.

"What she say?" Rigoret asked.

"Strong enough."

I clambered over her massive golden wing, trying not to think about how this trip might affect my dragon. Clarissima did not seem to have reservations; she nudged me gently with her huge tail, settling me on the scales just behind her neck ruff. The scales' ridges made them easy to grasp, if not that comfortable for sitting. But how often did I time-travel? I could handle the discomfort.

Rigoret was scowling even harder than usual. "I come!" he whispered. "Need me."

I ignored him as I anchored myself on Clarissima's back and tied a rope to her horns. "Go to Amma," I commanded, and doubled the rope around my wrists.

A surprisingly strong arm grabbed my waist just as Clarissima blinked us into the past.

I rolled off of Clarissima and threw up on the damp ground. Rigoret retched behind me, emptying his stomach of contents and then rolling away from the smelly pile. I crawled toward a tree on my hands and knees, desperate to get away from the odor lest my stomach try to turn my body inside out.

I reached out a hand and touched Clarissima's long snout. It was cold. Her snout was never cold. Lifting my aching head, I stared into her enormous whirling eyes.

"Clarissima! All right?" What if she were too weak to get us back home?

The response was slow in coming. *Will be. Need rest.*

I rolled my neck slowly, looking around. We were in an open space surrounded by heavily laden fruit trees. They were not there in our time, but I recognized the pond behind them, and even better, the mountain in the near distance. I gestured toward it with my chin.

"Your mountain. Safe?"

Clarissima turned her head and regarded the mountain. Her color shifted subtly in what I had come to recognize as positive emotion, maybe even joy.

My brother may still be there.

With an enormous heave she lifted into the sky, bending the fruit trees with the wind from her down draft. I watched her disappear into the shadow of the mountain, then lay on my back until I felt a little stronger. Rigoret was curled on his side.

"Never again," he wheezed out.

"Told you no!" I scratched my nose, hard. Rigoret said I always scratched my nose when I was angry. Maybe I did. I *was* angry at Rigoret for coming, but I understood. We were both anxious and wanted to do something. I consciously moved my hand away from my face and looked around.

The landscape was familiar, and not. In our time the path to the pond was overgrown with weeds—no one had gone there in annuals. The walk was too far and swimming took too much energy. Here, there was a grassy slope to the quiet water with a bench sitting near it. I puzzled over that. What was the purpose of a bench by the water? We worked and then we slept. No one would waste time sitting by the pond—if they could even get to it. It was too far from the village to even reach without riding a mule!

But at least I knew the village would be over the next rise and behind another stand of trees. It was a long walk— we had to get started. I nodded impatiently at Rigoret and pushed to my feet. We would need to rest along the way, and I hoped to at least see the village before nightfall.

I gasped as I fell to the ground behind an enormous oak. My legs were trembling and I was starving. It had taken us too long to get within sight of the village and I had made the route even longer in order to stay within cover. At least I *thought* we had to hide. No one I knew had ever time traveled before; I had not even known it was possible before Clarissima suggested it. But we were committed now.

Rigoret and I lay beside huge tree roots, sucking in air and trying to get the strength to…What? I had no idea what we should do next.

"Need food," whispered Rigoret. He rolled over onto his stomach and leaned around the base of the tree, peering through the dusk. He began dragging himself from tree trunk to tree trunk. We both assumed that, like in our time, a stand of trees circled our village and protected our garden and houses from the strong winds of winter. When we made our way to the last row of trees we would finally see what our village had looked like sixty annuals ago.

At the edge of the trees a huge garden stretched ahead of us, easily four times the size of one in our time. How many villagers did they have who could manage a garden this size? Had there been two villages back then, and now it had shrunk to one? The leaves looked a little dry and withered, as if there had not been enough water lately, and, when I leaned in to look more closely, I saw that there were more weeds than Amma would have allowed in our garden. But it was still the largest garden I had ever seen. And no stools.

I shook my head. This was a strange place. Was this really our village?

Rigoret's whistle, our signal for danger, snatched me from my reverie. I swung my head around, looking for him. He had crawled past me and was leaning against a shed on the edge of the garden,

WHAT IF IT KILLS YOUR DRAGON?

pointing at something with a shaking hand. I stood and walked toward him; it would have taken too long to crawl, and if there was something dangerous ahead, I needed to know about it now.

Collapsing against the shed, I tried to follow the line of his arm. The sun was dropping and even though I squinted hard, there seemed to be shadows everywhere. People were moving back and forth from the village meeting house, stepping around mounds on the ground.

I crawled forward, trying to see more clearly. Then it dawned on me that what I had taken for mounds of dirt were actually people—children?—lying on pallets on the ground. I tried to make sense of what I was seeing. Sleeping outside under the stars? Was their Celebration of the Great Mother outside rather than within the meeting place? The weather was a bit cool for that.

I watched as one of the adults bent and hugged a child to their chest. For the first time I heard the weeping, as if my ears had been broken and now suddenly worked.

I gasped, falling back against Rigoret. "Dead?"

"Dying, I think."

We slid back against the wall of the shed and watched as adults walked slowly between the rows of children, sometimes stroking, sometimes embracing, always crying. Then a woman wrapped in a long cloak emerged from the meeting place carrying a large pot. She drifted slowly down each row, cajoling each child to take a sip from the pot. She would bend and lift the child's head, quickly sliding a spoon between their lips and tilting the liquid down their throats. What had happened to the children? Had they gotten a disease from an animal or some stranger wandering through?

Rigoret and I looked at each other.

"Talk to Elder?" he asked.

I paused, considering. We had no idea what was going on. We also didn't know how long we would be able to stay here.

"Find Amma. Ask her."

Rigoret gave a short nod and started crawling. We both assumed Amma would be in the same house our family had lived in for generations. It was unfortunate that it was not right beside the gardens, but at least we knew where to go.

As we crawled and rested, crawled and rested, I worried about whether we might somehow become infected with this disease and bring more sickness back to our time rather than a cure. What if we encountered a purer form of the curse than we already had? What if everyone dropped dead once we returned? Our villagers were tired all of the time, but we did not have children stretched out on the ground. Well, we really had no children, but our youngest were not ill.

Did Rigoret and I need to spend the rest of our lives here to avoid killing everyone in our own time?

I blinked back tears. I was such an arrogant fool.

By the time we reached Amma's house Rigoret and I were so hungry we could have eaten blades of grass. It was full dark now, although lanterns had been lit around the village meeting house, and people were still moving back and forth among the children, covering them with blankets and stroking their heads.

Rigoret and I collapsed on our backs, resting before making the final push up the two stairs to Amma-three-times's back door. I gazed up at the sky, counting the stars and trying to calm myself. To not be able to see my Amma again…. For both Rigoret and me to disappear and not be there to help her as she became weaker and

54

weaker.... Or to not be able to take her to the Celebration of the Great Mother, which she loved and looked forward to each harvest! Tears slid down my cheeks into my ears. Perhaps we could find the cure and send it back by Clarissima. She at least would not be tainted. Please, Great Mother, make it so.

I sniffed hard and rolled over, preparing myself to rise. "Come."

Rigoret dutifully began to push up. He had said nothing since seeing the children. Perhaps we had both been dragged down into despair. But who knew? Perhaps this Amma would be able to help. I clutched at that hope.

Rigoret and I walked up the stairs to the back door and pulled the string that rang the small bell by the back door, causing me to smile when I heard the happy tingling sound, so much like the one from our own back door bell. I looked over at Rigoret, but he was gazing behind us at the shadows beneath the trees and the darkness crowding in. Shivering, I turned back to the door, which opened only wide enough for one hooded eye.

"Who are you?" The voice was raspy, but eerily familiar. How strange that Amma-three-times could sound so similar to her descendant so far removed.

"Your children four times," I whispered into the crack. "Us explain?"

The door did not budge.

"Whee-whaaed blankets," Rigoret murmured.

There was a cackle and the door swung open. Rigoret looked triumphantly at me and stepped inside. I followed, shaking my head. I had forgotten that Amma claimed that the saying had originated with Amma-three-times.

Amma-three-times looked so much like our Amma that at first I thought there had been some mistake and we had just been whisked back to our own time. But this Amma—this Amma was not wheezing and chained to her bed. This Amma scooted around us to shut the door, then grasped both our arms to tug us into the light from the fireplace, staring at us and gripping our wrists until they hurt.

"Who are you? Tell me the truth!"

"Selina is Amma-two-times," I whispered, "Then our Amma Dinat."

Amma-three-times shook her head. "That cannot be. That cannot...." She trailed off in a sob. "My Selina is lying on the ground, dying." She wrenched her hands free and fell into a rickety wooden chair, tears dropping into a cloth she pulled out of a large pocket.

I dropped onto my knees in front of her as Rigoret moved to her side and began rubbing her back in quick hard strokes.

"Amma. Selina lived. We time-travel." I paused to pull in air.

Rigoret picked up the story. "Selina our Amma-two-times," he added from behind her chair. "Mole on arm?"

And then Amma-three-times began weeping in huge wet bellowing wails that shook her body and squeezed my heart. I leaned my head against her knee and cried with her; I wasn't sure why. For the children withering on the ground and their terrified families? For my Amma, who was fading away? Or for myself and Rigoret and the young people of our village, who would watch our Ammas and Appas die and then lie down beside them?

Finally the sobs became sniffles and the sniffles reduced to nose blowing. Amma-three-times closed her eyes and leaned back against the chair, her chest occasionally heaving. I wiped my nose with the back of my hand and pushed myself up, walking to the kitchen in a house I could have navigated in complete darkness. The layout had not changed in sixty annuals, and the kitchen, which was the largest room in the house, had a huge hearth with an array of hooks and poles for hanging iron cookpots and skewering unlucky animals.

I hung a pot of water over the fire and found cups and loose tea, eying the shelves surreptitiously. Was there something we could eat? I had to eat soon or I would pass out right here on the kitchen floor.

"Amma," I began tentatively. "Food?"

She gestured vaguely at a shelf running over the big sink. I almost laughed. That was where we kept *our* cookie jar. I stepped up on the box pushed under the sink and pulled down the heavy jar, which turned out to be stuffed with my favorite oatmeal bars.

"Selina has not been eating them," Amma-three-times muttered. "Take as many as you want."

Rigoret and I sat on the kitchen floor, stuffing bars into our mouths as fast as we could swallow, almost choking on huge unchewed pieces. By the time we stopped smashing food into our mouths the jar was half empty. Now I needed something to drink. I rolled to my feet to check if the water was hot enough for tea.

What did we do now? So far we knew nothing that would help our village; in fact, now we had a new mystery. What was making the children sick? Had they somehow given a disease to their parents, and then recovered? How long could we even stay here, stumbling around, hoping an answer would fall on our heads?

I didn't realize I was standing stockstill, staring into the tea jar, until Amma-three-times brushed past me and gently pushed me out of the kitchen.

"We will all be in the arms of the Great Mother by the time your tea is made." She took the jar out of my hands and began moving around the kitchen at a speed I had never witnessed. Cooking was usually a slow, deliberate ritual, with frequent rest breaks on hard kitchen chairs. I plopped down on the floor by Rigoret and we both watched her in amazement. What would it mean to have this kind of strength? The things I could get done in a day!

"Amma," I began, "why children sick? And not you?"

Amma poured hot water into three cups. "It was sudden. Happened all at once." She talked without looking at us as she walked back to rehang the pot on the hook. "Only the children got sick— so sick…" Amma choked as she continued. "But no Ammas or Appas. No one understands why. No one has an answer. We meet and talk and scream and cry and nothing changes!" She covered her eyes and bent over, almost too close to the fire.

We must go. Clarissima's voice sounded strained.

I clutched Rigoret's arm. "Clarissima calling! Go back."

Rigoret shook his head vehemently. "Know nothing!"

"What week this?" I asked Amma-three-times urgently.

She turned toward me, frowning a bit as a huge thump rattled the house. "End of Harvest Moon," Amma said slowly, holding two steaming cups of tea. "But please tell me more of Selina and your Amma. I am anxious to know. Are there many little ones?"

I stood, pulling a reluctant Rigoret to his feet. "Try return. Beginning of Raining Moon. Must go."

Rigoret dragged his feet as I pushed him toward the door, but he moved a little faster when Clarissima once again banged her tail on the ground and shook the house. Amma-three-times looked puzzled until she glanced out the kitchen window—even in the dark one could see the glow from Clarissima's body and make out the display of color.

"A dragon! So you *did* come from the future," she acknowledged, as if she had still been uncertain up until now. "And you will come back?"

"Yes!" Rigoret promised, as if Clarissima would follow his directions. I tried to smile reassuringly, but what if we couldn't? What if Clarissima didn't have the strength?

We shuffled down the stairs and dragged ourselves across the small yard to where she lay, heaving, on the cold ground. Even in the semi-dark I could see that her colors were muted.

I bit my lip as I pulled Rigoret up behind me onto Clarissima's back. And then we were gone.

I threw myself onto the ground, refusing to vomit up those oatmeal bars. I was sure they would not taste as good the second time. Rigoret lay beside me, both of us swallowing convulsively to stop the upward movement of food. Finally our stomachs quieted down and I pushed myself upright.

My stomach might be full of my favorite sweet snack, but it still felt as if pointed sticks were stabbing my belly. If the illness only affected children, and we didn't have any children, then we should not be able to infect anyone. Right?

Then why did I feel as if we should run away and live by ourselves in a forest? Were we making things worse or better?

I rubbed my hands over my face. At least the children in the beforetimes had lived. And since everyone in our village was already dying, how could we really make things worse?

I breathed in long and consciously relaxed my shoulders. We had to continue to look for a cure.

I slid a gentle hand onto Clarissima's snout. If it had been cold before, it was freezing now. I snatched my hand away, leaning down to look straight into her eyes.

"Be all right?"

Clarissima's mind rumble was faint. *Yes. Did you find what you needed?*

I paused. Should I tell the truth? But what would I gain by lying? I had to know if she could do it one more time. We just didn't have enough information.

"Can...Can go back once more?" It was a long sentence, but I had to know.

Clarissima's irises whirled as she stared at me. *Once more only.*

It took her two tries to heave herself into the air. That had never happened before.

My only friend. She was my only friend. I dropped my head, tears in my eyes.

"Well?" Rigoret asked.

I picked at a scab on my arm, not wanting to look at him. He would certainly sacrifice Clarissima to save our village. Would I? Should I?

"Well?" he asked again, a little louder.

I held up one finger. Once more. One more time. We had to make it count.

We sat by Amma's bed, telling her about our trip. She frowned when we described children lying on pallets on the ground and smiled at "whee-whaaed blankets". But she said nothing, too exhausted to even offer advice. When we finished talking she nodded minutely and closed her eyes.

We slid quietly from her room and pulled the curtain across her doorway. What to do now?

"Get information," Rigoret announced firmly.

I agreed. We would use this time to find out everything we could about illnesses that only attacked children. Clearly Amma-two-times, Selina, had been cured, because she had lived to raise our Amma. So what was the point of us rushing around and looking for a cure for the children's illness?

But what if she was cured *because* of us?? What if we were the ones who brought back the cure and all the children would die if we didn't go back one more time?

I pushed up and went to stare out the window. We could be making things worse. We could be saving lives. I didn't know what was right. When Rigoret made up his mind about something, he refused to consider any other course. I loved my younger brother, but he was not someone I could discuss options with. I had no one. So I would just do my best. We would gather information and go back one more time—we had to learn how the children were cured and the adults became ill.

Rigoret and I woke the next morning, cooked first meal for ourselves and Amma, and planned as we ate. No one we knew had time-traveled before and I wasn't sure I wanted others to know. But how to get the answers we needed without giving away that we knew things no one else did?

"Read in book?" Rigoret asked, munching on his overly toasted bread. I still had not gotten the knack of holding the bread over the fire just long enough for it to turn golden brown, like Amma did. I always got distracted and only saved the slices once they smelled and looked burnt.

I shook my head as I scraped some of the black from my bread and sat opposite him at the small table. Everyone knew I liked to read the stories in the weekly and saved them to reread, but I had never read anything about villages mourning because all of their children were dying.

"Green Oaks Village?" I suggested. "Check children sick?"

Rigoret shrugged. "We visit village."

"Yellow Bush Village?"

He finished his bread and licked his fingers. The boy loved bread! Slowly, he shook his head. "Too far. Worry about here."

I nodded. We could visit the closest village and see if all their children had ever been ill. But first we could try to get more information here.

Together we cleaned the kitchen and then made our way to the house of the First Elder. She was frail and near death, and I regretted imposing on her, but maybe she could tell us something that would help. The First Elder's home was a little larger than that of the other villagers, with a high fence around her garden behind the house. Many villagers' gardens had fences, as the deer and raccoons loved to wander into the village and enjoy easy pickings. It was First Elder's tonics and brews that healed us when we became ill, so it made sense that her garden would need to be a little larger.

I frowned at myself. Why was I wondering about these things now? I was picking at loose leaves, as Amma would say. I'd never been quite sure what that meant.

As usual, the First Elder's daughter came to the door and ushered us into the front room. No, we could not speak directly to the Elder, but Senta would convey our questions to her. We waited anxiously as Senta walked to the back of the house, moving with the usual hitch in her step. The village rumor was that it was from a hip injury she'd had when she was small, but I had never had the courage to ask if that was true. I had never had the courage to talk much to her at all—I had never spoken with Senta outside of this house. She rarely left her mother's side, never visited anyone in the village—I didn't think I had ever seen her smile.

Nevertheless, Senta's movements were mesmerizingly graceful, and I had tried many times to mimic sliding across the floor the way she did.

Too soon, Senta was gliding back into the front room. "Amma only knows 'red bumps'." Pause. Deep breath. "But all children death disease? No."

She was talking to the floor; Senta never looked us in the eye or seemed to connect with anyone at all. I always wondered about her life. She had no friends and tended a mother who had been ill and near the Great Mother for as long as I had been alive. It always seemed so sad.

"Which village?" she asked.

"Yellow Bush." I hoped she didn't ask me any further questions.

She nodded, then focused once more on her feet. "Tonight Celebration of Great Mother." Pause for breath. "Be well."

So that was it. The signal to leave. Rigoret and I stood and left the house. I frowned as we walked to the cart. Was Amma strong enough for the Celebration? No one ever missed the Celebration. Ever. But she was so weak.

I bit the inside of my cheek. One issue at a time. Next step: visit another village.

We rode into the market, asking a woman on the street about the doctor. She spoke in long phrases that made me tired just listening to her, but we finally discovered that the doctor's office was next to one of the flower stalls.

The doctor, who I thought was rather young—didn't you need to be stooped and have gray hair in order to really have knowledge?—was not helpful at all. He barely listened to us and rushed us out of his office once he found out neither of us were paying patients. But his assistant (who did have gray hair!) was very kind, and gave us a pot of ointment for children with rash and a bottle of blue liquid for "general health." She shook her head and said she had never heard the like when we said all the children were dying but none of the adults. And she dabbed at her eyes as she walked us to the door. I was grateful for her. Maybe the ointment and the drink would help in some way. Maybe.

The closest village was laid out like ours, with the village meeting place in the center and the houses arranged in a semicircle with their gardens behind and in-between. Everyone was moving briskly about: working in the gardens, building a new house under the trees, sitting at a table drinking tea. They all looked well and happy, and we could see the children bustling about doing chores or sneaking off to play.

Finally a young man holding a rake sauntered up to our cart, looking us up and down as if we were not worth his time.

"Mother bless you," I muttered, having trouble looking directly at him. He seemed to be pulsing with energy. I studied my hands, heavy on my thighs. "Help us?"

Rigoret leaned forward, taking over. "Children all sick?"

The young man waved at the children bouncing about, laughing and teasing each other. His impatient look hardened.

"But beforetimes?" I asked desperately.

"Why are you wasting my time?" He turned back toward the tumbling children, walking away without another word.

Rigoret's usual scowl looked even more fierce. "Why just us?"

I shook my head, lost in thought as I turned our mule towards our village. Everyone drank the same water and surely was eating the same food. One or two children might experiment with a strange plant in the forest, but never all of them! Had the children been cursed, and somehow it had moved from them to the adults? I twirled a curl around my finger, tugging on it as I thought.

I sat up straighter. Somehow the children must have been cured, because Amma-two-times Selina had lived and had children. Rigoret and I could not have gone back and helped everyone—all we had was a jar of ointment and some strange drink that the doctor's assistant said would not cure a disease. I looked doubtfully at the bottle of blue liquid. What would this stuff even do?

If we wanted answers, Rigoret and I needed to travel back to a later time when the children had revived and their cure could be used for their parents.

I brushed aside small issues like: why hadn't it happened this way the first time? Surely when adults began getting sick, the first recourse would have been to use whatever had cured the children. But maybe there had been a gap in time between when the children were restored to health and when their parents became ill, and the recipe for the medicine had been lost.

When I relayed my theory to Rigoret it made even less sense than it had in my head. For something as terrifying as every child becoming deathly ill, no one would forget to document the remedy. But Rigoret agreed that we had to go back to the time after the children had been cured. Even if it did not cure her, the medicine they had used might at least help our Amma. We were desperate. It was all up to Clarissima...

...who moved as if she were weighted with rocks. Her long tail lay compressed against the ground, its perpetual movement arrested. She dragged her head toward me, echoing the mini-movements of Amma, caught in her own decomposition in the house close by. Amma didn't have long—Rigoret knew it, I knew it, and Amma knew it. I thought she might be hanging on to attend one more Celebration. She had always loved them so. But our neighbor Jolet could be trusted to watch over Amma for us, and we had to take *some* action.

From the looks of her, Clarissima didn't have long, either. A sob caught in my throat.

I dropped onto the ground and pulled the tip of her snout into my lap. "Too weak for jump?"

Rigoret stood behind her with his arms crossed.

I can do it. We cannot stay long.

"What she say?" Rigoret demanded. "Must go! Give Amma-three-times ointment." Deep breath. "And drink!" He dropped to his knees, balancing with his hands, then once again crossing his arms. "Talk to First Elder." Breath. "May have solution!" The tears in his eyes belied his angry stance.

I can do it. Clarissima repeated.

I gritted my teeth and nodded. "All right. Back by Celebration," I added to Clarissima.

Long before, she agreed.

Rigoret and I climbed onto her wide back, tucking away the jar of ointment and bottle of blue tonic from the doctor's assistant. I held on tightly to the rope tied to her horns and Rigoret held on tightly to me, until we were hit with the disorienting blast of light and dizziness and we both rolled, retching, off her back.

"Must hurry," I wheezed. My ankles hurt, my knees ached, my lower back creaked as I pushed to my knees. Clarissima did not move, just lay there on the ground, her skin pale, her huge chest heaving. I ran my fingers down her scales and on impulse took out the tonic.

"For Selina!" groaned Rigoret, his hands still wrapped around his unsettled stomach.

"A drop," I snapped, then turned to Clarissima. "Open."

Her cavernous mouth, full of teeth the length of my longest finger stretched open wide enough for me to tip a few drops of the blue tonic onto her long flat tongue. She clamped her mouth shut. Her entire body shuddered.

What is that? A bit of color surfaced in her scales and her eyes regained their whirling prisms.

I shrugged my shoulders. "Tonic from doctor."

"Huh. Looks better," Rigoret commented. He crawled closer to us.

"Open up," I demanded Clarissima, and then tipped another careful drop onto her tongue. Once again she shuddered but revived a bit more.

"Go rest," I commanded as I shoved to standing. "Need to take to children."

But this time it wasn't Amma's bleary eye that stared at us through the crack in the door. It was a young girl's.

Rigoret was quicker than I was. "Selina?"

The cracked widened. "You are from the future! Like Amma said!!"

The door was flung open and small arms hugged me, then Rigoret.

"Amma said you would come back!" She was beautiful, even though her bony arms and legs had dry, scaly patches. "Come, come! Now Amma needs you!"

We followed Amma-two-times, Selina, into the small house, both throwing questions at her as fast as we could breathe.

"How healed?"

"How Amma sick?"

"All children well?"

"When healed?"

Selina laughed and led us back to Amma's room, where she abruptly grew serious. "Is this your illness?"

We stood by Amma-three-time's bed, appalled. When we had visited before she had been energetic and tireless— now she resembled our Amma, exhausted and wasting away.

Rigoret nodded as I pulled the tonic out of my coat. He gently slid his arm underneath Amma's shoulders and held her up.

"Wait!" Selina was not as comfortable with us as she had seemed. "What are you doing?" She tried to block our access to Amma, but it was too late. We were bigger than she was and we were in a hurry.

"Good for her," I said soothingly as I tipped a few drops into Amma's mouth. She swallowed slowly as Rigoret lowered her gently onto the bed.

Gradually, Amma's eyes fluttered open. "Ahhhhh," she exhaled. "Better."

She saw Rigoret and me and smiled, then openly grinned when she spied Selina standing just behind us.

"My Selina. Healthy. Just as you said." The smile faded as she turned toward the wall. "But you must leave now. Go back to your time."

Rigoret and I both shook our heads vehemently. "What happened?" he demanded.

"How Selina heal?" I followed up.

Amma shook her head. "Go home. Our children will live."

"But you! Our Amma," I pleaded desperately. "Please. Dying."

Amma again shook her head.

I scratched my nose hard as I shoved away from the bed. "Talk to First Elder."

"No!" Amma shot up into a sitting position. "You must not. Promise me."

Rigoret adopted his usual stubborn stance, his arms across his chest. "Why?"

But my mind was elsewhere. If Amma-three-times was that adamant about us not talking to the First Elder, then she must know something important. I was glad that Amma had her daughter back, but I wanted my mother to live. I headed for the door with Rigoret a step behind me. Selina ran and tried to hold us back but she was no match for the two of us. Rigoret lifted her gently and set her to the side.

We only had a short time here, so I handed the ointment to Selina as we closed the door behind us and said, "Tell Amma we love her. Always." I considered giving Selina the tonic, but we might need it for Clarissima to get us home. And—I hated to be so selfish—for our Amma.

It was dusk, but we knew where the home of the First Elder was. We lived in this village, after all. But there were no carefully distanced stools to sit on, so we had to stop and lean on one another when we needed to rest.

As we crossed the center green, the door to the house of the First Elder opened and a cloaked figure emerged, a large hood trimmed in fur over her head.

One spurt of energy and we would be close enough to talk. Surely she knew what had cured the children. And even what was now poisoning the adults. Maybe she would recognize this tonic if it had been around long enough. She must have some answers! But our pace was so slow. The time travel had drained Rigoret and me as well as Clarissima.

I frowned as I watched the First Elder's progress toward the meeting house. There was something peculiar about that gait....

Must. Go. Now.

I grabbed Rigoret's arm. "Clarissima says must go now."

Rigoret snatched his arm away. "Need answers!"

"One more minute?" I asked Clarissima desperately. I tried to hurry toward the First Elder.

Even Clarissima's mind voice was faint. *Now.*

I lunged again for Rigoret's arm. "Go now!!!" I turned and began dragging him back in the direction from which we had come. "Amma needs us."

At that, Rigoret stopped fighting me and tromped beside me.

We had been so close! I realized that I was dragging my feet and tried to move more quickly. But my stomach clenched. My head hurt. The answers were here.

We rounded the corner of the house and there lay Clarissima, once more still and flaccid. I poured a few drops onto her tongue and climbed onto her back, Rigoret behind me.

Until he jumped off. Just as Clarissima and I were swallowed by color.

The last few seconds were like barreling through a wall. When we finally landed on the ground behind our house, Clarissima had streaks of purple blood along her sides. My body felt as if it had been mashed through a pipe—I would have bruises along both arms and legs and my ears were ringing. Or maybe that was because I was screaming Rigoret's name.

I had left my brother in the past. I would never see him again.

I rolled off of Clarissima's back, dry heaved, then crawled to her face. She had left my brother, my only brother behind. But the streaks of bloody pus running from her eyes and nose, the ragged tears along her side and the halting breaths gave me pause. I rested my forehead on one tattered wing and just let the tears flow. For her. For Rigoret. For Amma. For me.

Finally she whispered, *Must go to my mountain. I can heal there.*

"Are you sure?" I stroked her wing gently where the skin did not seem abraded, then pulled the bottle out of my pocket. "Will more tonic help?"

Beware that tonic. It contains life and comes from living things.

"I...What?"

But Clarissima said no more, and after several tries she lifted her body into the air and slowly made her way toward her mountain.

I let myself into our house. Without Rigoret. How would I be able to explain this to Amma?

How could I live with myself?

The house was so quiet. Tears trickled down my cheeks as I slid into Amma's bedroom. Her bed was empty—Mothers help us! Had Jolet already taken her to the Celebration? We must have returned later than I thought. Clarissima must not have been well enough to calibrate the time precisely.

I sighed as I sat down heavily on Amma's bed. How could I go to the Celebration when Rigoret was stranded? I had to get Clarissima well enough to take me back and rescue him. Perhaps Rigoret could go to Amma-three-times' house and wait there with Selina until I could get back.

I dragged myself to standing. I would attend the Celebration—not going was not an option. And when Amma asked me where Rigoret was, I would tell her—what? That she would never see him again?

Clarissima would just have to jump one more time. Even though the last one had almost killed her.

71

If she didn't, Amma would die and my brother would be gone forever and I would be alone until the disease took me, too.

It was quiet on the green. The moon was already high in the sky and the comfortable dark settled around me. I must have missed the singing and dancing and feasting part of the Celebration. Well, not so much singing and dancing these days. But it was fortunate that I was coming in when things were winding down. Fewer conversations, less explaining. Now everyone was probably bedded down for the community sleep, which had always been the highlight for me. How fun to sleep together with everyone from the village, like one big family! Share the cup, snuggle into the cozy blanket, and slide into sweet dreams with all of your neighbors. And wake up to a huge community breakfast before returning to your home with a warm feeling of belonging. Except for the part about everyone being weak and exhausted, despite the long sleep.

I stopped to rest on one of the stools, soothed by the night breeze. I would get Rigoret back. And when I returned for him, we would force answers from the First Elder, no matter what Amma-three-times said.

The meeting place had big windows that were open to the sweet night air. I could see everyone stretched out on their pallets, an uncomfortable reminder of the sick children of sixty annuals past. And Senta, with that hitch in her step, was walking down the rows of my neighbors, placing something on each person's stomach.

I shot up, trying to better see what was happening. Fighting against my exhaustion, I stepped forward, staying in the shadows, sliding to the window to sneak a peek.

Seeds. She was placing big white seeds on each person and then each seed was slowly turning blue!

I frowned as I watched Senta slide to the next person, walking just like…just like the First Elder sixty annuals ago!

Were those seeds healing our people or making them sicker?

She moved closer to where I could see Amma resting. She was *not* going to put that thing on my Amma! Because Amma certainly was not getting any better.

I pulled out the tonic and took a few sips. Ahhhh. I felt stronger. I walked quickly to the door of the meeting house and threw it open. Senta looked up at me, pausing in her careful placement of seeds on everyone's bellies, seeds turning a bright indigo as my neighbors' breathing hitched and grew more shallow.

"Step away from my Amma," I ground out.

I jumped across two neighbors and tackled Senta. If I was wrong I would have to leave my village. But somehow I knew I was right. Senta, whose distinctive walk I had recognized in the past, had been First Elder sixty annuals ago, and she was killing our village with these strange seeds.

Senta backhanded me so hard I was knocked back over a row of sleepers. She was so strong! My head slapped the ground and my vision blurred, but she was not going to kill my Amma!

I crawled up and over the sleepers, but instead of trying to hit Senta, I swung for the bag at her hip, knocking seeds everywhere.

Senta screeched, diving at me and banging my head against the ground. I tried to push her away, but I was dizzy and my movements lacked the force of hers. All I could see were her wild black eyes and thin, wet lips hanging over my face. I kneed her in her stomach but she just grunted and went for my throat.

Great Mother, I would die here and when Amma woke up, both Rigoret and I would be gone.

Two huge hands reached around Senta, pulled her off me and threw her across the room.

I blinked at the stranger as I tried to pull in a much-needed breath. Who was this?

Another man, older, knelt beside me. There were tears in his eyes. "Leena," he whispered, and pulled me into his arms.

I was in too much pain to resist. "Who are you?" I rasped.

He smiled. "Don't you recognize your brother?"

He nodded at my rescuer, now aided by another young man and woman, immobilizing a shrieking Senta. "My children." A huge grin stretched across his face.

What had happened to the grumpy, stubborn Rigoret?

"She has the strength of ten, Appa!" yelled the young woman.

"You can handle her," Rigoret replied without turning around. "I am with my sister."

"Help me up," I wheezed. "I can't hug you like this." The tears were running so thickly down my cheeks that everything was a blur. Could this be true? How could Rigoret have grown children? In just one day?

A short woman with hair tied away from a kind face squatted beside us. "Sweet greetings, sister," she began, "but we think we need to remove the seed balls on everyone. Is that all right with you?"

"Yes! Making ill!" I made sure there was no seed on Amma's body. Throughout the fighting and screaming, none of the sleeping villagers had stirred. So Senta had drugged us every year?

The woman moved quickly to gather up the seeds, handling the indigo ones especially carefully and placing them on a tray.

Rigoret's children had tied up Senta, who continued to rant and curse at us, our Ammas, and even the Great Mother.

I leaned against Rigoret, closing my eyes and so grateful that I was able to see him again. Even if he now looked old enough to be my Appa-three-times!

He murmured in my ear, "That is Hapta, my children's Amma. We have been together for almost forty annuals." Rigoret shook his head and clutched me even more closely. "Leena. I can't believe I am finally seeing you again." Tears matching mine ran down his face.

An old woman leaning on a cane walked slowly into the meeting house. Hapta ran to get her a chair as the three adult children dragged the howling, writhing Senta toward her. Rigoret gently helped me up and we tottered toward the group. I was grateful for the chair that Hapta pushed toward me with a smile, almost falling into it.

For a moment we all studied Senta, who continued to screech and rave until the old woman nodded at the younger and pronounced, "Enough."

The young woman tore a strip from her skirt and tied it around Senta's mouth. The sudden silence reverberated around the big room. I pushed back in the chair and let the pain of my body wash over me. I was so tired.

The old woman might look frail, but her voice was strong. "First Elder Senta," she almost spat, "you have shamed us all with your witchcraft. You are an abomination. But you are not our first concern now." She turned to the young woman and Rigoret. "We must save these villagers. Go to her garden. Those blue seeds grew something. Handle the seeds carefully and pull up whatever blue plants you find, for those contain their souls."

My head snapped up. What? Senta had been bleeding us of our *souls*? I tried to push myself out of the chair, but everything hurt.

One of the young men stationed himself by the old woman's chair. "I will stay by you, Amma-two-times. In case she somehow gets free."

The old woman patted his hand fondly as the others started for the door.

"Wait. Please wait for me," I pleaded.

Rigoret turned back. "I would never leave you," he smirked as he picked me up.

"But I...," I sputtered, "*You* jumped off Clarissima!"

Rigoret laughed, a deep, wonderful sound I had not heard in years, even before he left. "Yes. And it was the best thing I ever did!"

"Indeed," Hapta agreed from his other side.

The two children smiled at each other as they opened the door and we headed across the green to the First Elder's home. Partway there I insisted on trying to walk by myself. I ended up leaning heavily on Hapta, and having to pause every few steps to catch my breath, but everyone was patient as we progressed slowly through the shadowed village.

I had never been past the front parlor of the First Elder's house...which was apparently Senta's house, because there was no First Elder who was in the bed close to death. So Senta had been First Elder for eighty annuals? Somehow she must have made herself look as if she were aging at first, then pretended to be her own daughter. How had we all been so blind?

And the house! Beyond the front parlor was a house filled with riches I could never have even imagined. Intricately made furniture, thick carpets, exquisite crockery. The lanterns had colored glass that would no doubt cast multi colored images on walls painted in soft colors. I was stunned at the magnificence of this home right in the midst of our humble village. The cloth at our own windows had been mended many times; our chairs were rough and hard, and the bedding we slept on scratchy and thin. This kind of opulence— where had these riches come from?

But the most important thing was saving our neighbors, so even though everyone was gasping at its grandeur, we walked straight through the house into a garden filled with flowers in all shades of blue. A sea of flowers, some as high as my shoulders, waving in the night breeze.

"Pull them gently from the root," Hapta instructed. "These flowers have grown from the souls of the villagers. But you must capture the complete plant--anything left growing will continue to eat their souls."

I turned to look at her. How did she know all this? Hapta stood tall amidst flowers the color of a summer sky, the moon reflecting in her eyes. Here was my image of the Great Mother. Strong. Nurturing. Protective.

She caught my stare and smiled gently. "Let us save your neighbors. My Amma is First Elder. She will explain everything when we return to the meeting house."

Rigoret's daughter disappeared back into the house and returned with two huge bags from the kitchen. "Left broken crockery all over the floor," she remarked with satisfaction.

She handed a bag to her brother and crouched on the ground, gently working a brilliant blue flower out of the ground. I moved away from her and sat, slowly pulling on the flowers near me. Hapta gathered them in mounds around us, going back in the house to dump kitchen supplies on the floor and garner more bags. So many flowers. So much pain.

We worked slowly and methodically across the field. Leena—
it turned out Rigoret had named his daughter after me—raided the
kitchen for cooked food, and brought out delicate pastries and
sliced meats we had never tasted before. There was even a pitcher
of the blue tonic, which boosted everyone's endurance. Even so,
the sun was rising by the time we had cleared the large garden.

I had had to stop and rest, leaning against the garden wall. Even
with the tonic every part of my body hurt, but I was so excited.
What would happen when we took the flowers back to the villagers? I didn't know the next step, but…Amma would be saved!
Wouldn't she? My Amma would live and Rigoret was still in my
life. I would not be alone.

Rigoret dropped down beside me, and we watched as Hapta,
who seemed to have the endurance of ten people, and her children
carried the flowers out of the garden to the meeting house. When
the last bundle was taken, Rigoret helped me to rise and I began
the task of hobbling back to the meeting house.

We opened the door to find the old woman snoring gently in
her chair as Rigoret's son sat on the floor, leaning against her leg.
He nodded sleepily to us and waved at Senta, whose eyes were slit-
ted with hate as the flowers were carried in.

Hapta gently awakened her mother. The old woman blinked
bleary eyes before focusing on the pile of flowers on the floor, then
turned to glare at Senta. I settled on the floor beside Amma's pallet.
"Do we make the flowers into a tonic?"

The old woman shook her head. "Where is my morning tea,
Leena?" Her voice was weak and querulous.

I stared at her. I was supposed to make morning tea?

Rigoret's daughter opened the door of the meeting house, a
steaming mug in her hand. Right. We had the same name. This

would get confusing. Rigoret must have thought he would never see me again.

Sniffing back tears, I watched and waited. Around me, our neighbors were stretching and blinking their eyes. But the stretches were slow and awkward. Even though they were awakening from a long night's sleep, everyone was still listless and weary.

Jolet sat up and pointed, alarmed at the sight of Senta bound and gagged. I rushed to explain.

"Neighbors! Senta cursed us." Deep breath. "She made us...." I paused. Would anyone believe she had been harvesting our souls? "...weak. This First Elder from...," I stopped again. I didn't know where any of them were from.

Rigoret picked up my speech. "Four villages over. She is here to help us."

Rigoret's children were walking between the rows, placing a blue flower beside each pallet. There were enough for each person, with some left over. I frowned at the number. Were those from neighbors who had died because they were so weak?

I realized that I was viciously scratching my nose. I stopped and rested my hand on Amma's arm. She was just now waking up, and smiled when she saw me.

The First Elder began speaking. Her voice was no longer querulous, but strong and commanding. "You have been poisoned by this one." Her foot pointed at Senta, who was lying still on the floor, staring at the ceiling. "You must take the flowers lying beside you and eat the petals. This is the cure for your strange illness."

Villagers turned to look at me, doubtful about following such a strange command from an outsider. I was the only familiar person sitting up—no one recognized Rigoret.

"Yes. Do this." I picked up the flower placed beside me and nibbled a bit from a petal. I moaned at the sense of...completion.

I gobbled down the rest of the petal and began on the next one. Sweet Mother! Delight surged through me. Elation. I realized that I was laughing as I savored each of the dark blue petals.

Laughter echoed all around me as neighbors followed my lead. I felt so good. So strong. I picked up Amma's flower and urged her to take a bite. Hesitantly, she nibbled a bit before grabbing the petal from me and taking huge bites.

And then she sat up! My Amma sat up.

Rigoret, his family, our Amma, the First Elder and I sat on Senta's plush furniture. Amma and I couldn't stop smiling. I guess because we all felt so *good*. Strong. Healthy. Energetic. I had never felt this whole in my entire life.

The First Elder was explaining how it had taken the Elders from across the land many annuals to figure out what was happening in our village. First they had to decide that there was something that merited investigating, overcoming the reluctance of Elders to interfere in other villages, then they had to believe that kind of evil was actually taking place. Even then, no one knew how to find a cure. Finally, a long-lost myth had been discovered and they had learned the story of the soul stealers. The first souls had to be freely given, which was why Senta had to poison the children and hold them hostage until the parents agreed to have their souls harvested. That one agreement held for all the generations to follow.

"Why didn't you come home before today, Rigoret?" I couldn't get over his grown children and full life he'd lived without me. And how had I said all that without gasping for breath?

"Clarissima said I had to wait until this Celebration of the Great Mother. I could not meet my former self. When we finally found out what to do we delayed until I could come. I would not let them visit you without me."

Amma kept shaking her head. She still could not believe that this grown man was Rigoret. I squeezed her hand. I could not believe it, either.

"We must ensure that no seeds are left behind to drain anyone's power," finished the First Elder.

Rigoret and I grinned at each other. Earlier, I had invited a revitalized Clarissima to use her firepower. Burning embers were all that remained of Senta's garden.

III

Terminal Freight

Dean Radt

Burning embers were all that remained of Pade's patience. His tolerance of people had been a charred wisp for so long that he'd grown used to it. He couldn't remember feeling otherwise, but the lying and the cheating he'd encountered in his short time on Varen-4 was fast burning away what little lenience he had left. Varen-4, that fleck of caustic bile in the galaxy. Always showing its ass to its sun.

"Mind saying that again?" Pade asked the scrawny man through gritted teeth. "I don't think I heard you right." He and the man squinted against the combined blaze of the sun and the glare reflecting off the ship's cargo ramp. Dust whirled and stuck to the sweat dripping down their faces and streaking their shirts.

The leathery farmer twisted and squeezed a dirty rag in his hands. His eyes shifted from the port's concrete floor to Pade's chest and back to the floor. "Um. We hate this too," he said with dry, cracked lips. "We're just not ready to ship, and clause thirteen-B in the contract allows us four hours to back out."

"I know what thirteen-B says. But you swore your group had eight tons of raw ore and five tons of processed norge stalks packaged, crated, and ready to ship."

"Um. Yeah, but—"

"I turned down three jobs." Pade held up three fingers and poked the man's chest with them. "Three, because you swore you wouldn't back out." It was a lie, but he hoped it would guilt the man into keeping to the contract.

The man looked up, pleading. "Maybe you could—"

"No! That ain't happening. They've already secured other haulers." Pade was angry enough to bust the swindler's nose, and it would feel so satisfying too. The thing that stayed his fist was his aversion to serving time in one of the planet's local jails, or its orbital prison. It wasn't the incarceration itself that he wished to avoid. It was that such a sentence would keep him tied to this rock, this non-revolving planet he was fast learning to loathe.

"I don't know what else to say," the man said.

"Say this was all a bad joke." Pade forced a smile and held his arms out, open, inviting good news.

It didn't come.

"Good luck, Mr. Deckard." The man backed away several steps before turning, mopping his brow with the dirty rag, and heading through one of the doors to the streets beyond.

Pade had spent all day trying to secure a client. A few had expressed interest in shipping their product off the planet, but none had signed a contract. This man and his local consortium were the best chance they'd had of getting paid to leave this craggy curse of a place.

He stepped off the ramp, staring at the oil-stained sandstone walls that formed the landing bay around his ship. Outside the port, things were not much better: just more weather-sculpted stone walls and sand and dust. The mining prospects were decent if you could tolerate the conditions, but one had to be part of a consortium to grow anything here. It took money to build a proper greenhouse.

Pade looked up at his ship. She'd always been pristine and beautiful in his mind, but now he noticed the scrapes and gouges from space debris and the rocks kicked up while approaching landing pads. On top of that, her hull was marked with entry and exhaust burns, fluid leaked from the landing struts, and the white paint was graying.

And his knee was hurting again.

"Shit!"

The next day Pade *let* Gater, his partner, head out to secure a client while he busied himself with ship maintenance. The day pressed on, and he received no updates. It seemed Gater was having as much trouble as Pade had had the day before.

Pade was kneeling in the shade at the top of the cargo ramp, lubricating the loading system's bearings, rollers, and joints, and was almost ready to run it through a test when Gater stepped onto the ramp. Behind him were three people.

The first was a pale, angular man in a dark suit, holding a black leather attaché case. He was about as tall as Gater, perhaps just shy of a hundred-eighty centimeters, placing him nine or ten centimeters shorter than Pade, and he appeared to be somewhere between Pade's thirty-three years of age and Gater's twenty-seven. Under the suit, the man wore a white shirt and a thin, copper-colored necktie, no doubt made of Ulaco silk. The shining metallic cloth was all the fashion on the primary planets but seldom seen in remote systems like this. The suit's short, perfectly sculpted hair boasted of an affluent lifestyle, the opposite of Gater's unkempt brown mop. He paused as he stepped onto the ramp, scanning the interior as though he were inspecting it.

The two following him, a man and a woman, didn't hesitate as they stepped aboard. Both were dressed casually, but Pade noticed their oversized, unzipped jackets, athletic physiques, and *don't-try-me* looks. It all told him something unpleasant might be coming.

Pade stood as the group approached. He wished he'd not worn his coveralls. The pistol on his belt was still reachable, but the garment would hamper its draw. Between him and his partner, Pade was the one who preferred his street clothes, and he always left the ship armed, just in case. Gater's training, experience with electrical equipment, and doctorates in astrophysics and astrofore (or fold mathematics) were a handicap when it came to anything violent. The engineer's outfit of choice was his mechanic's grease-stained coveralls and frayed tool belt. He was unarmed and would be of no help if things got spicy.

When Gater had left the ship earlier that morning, he'd looked uncomfortable in his button-down shirt and travel pants. He appeared absolutely miserable now as he led the strangers onto the ramp. Neither the suit, the man, nor the woman smiled. Their faces wore business like warpaint. Further indicators that something was off.

The man following the suit was burly. Thick neck. Thick arms. The latter filled out the sleeves of his bulky jacket, and he reminded Pade of a military K-9. He and Pade may have shared the same short haircut and sharp jawline, but the man obviously spent more time in the gym than Pade did. "Muscles" stopped at the bottom of the ramp and kept watch from that position, scanning the landing pad and the host of refuelers, maintenance personnel, and supply skids moving about.

The woman, walking right behind the suit, stared up the ramp at Pade. She was attractive and, like Pade, had tanned, weather-worn skin. He smiled, giving her his signature charm. Her grim demeanor did not change. Yeah, something was definitely off.

Halfway up the ramp, Gater started to speak. "Pade, this—"

The suit cut him off, brushing past Gater and offering his hand. "Paden Deckard, I'm Simon Smith. I represent your next fare."

Pade didn't like this man, both because of how he treated Gater and because he seemed so confident they would take the job. Both Pade and Gater had to accept a commission. That was their agreement, and Gater's apparent misery let Pade know this man would get two "piss off"s. Besides, no cargo, no destination, and no pay had been discussed. Not paid meant no Pade.

He dropped the rag he'd been holding and reached out with his grease-smeared hand. He didn't want to shake the man's hand, but the opportunity to get grease on him or his pompous suit was too tempting.

Smith's eyes swept over Pade. He cocked his head and turned without shaking his hand, motioning to the woman beside him and the man at the bottom of the ramp. Pade's greasy outstretched hand hung in the air.

"These are my associates, Alex and Kelly," Smith stated. The woman eyed Pade. The man at the bottom of the ramp maintained his focus on the port.

Pade brought his hand down and wiped both of them on his coveralls, wondering who was who but realizing it didn't matter. He didn't like either of them. The woman watched him intently, focusing on his hands. Her right hand moved toward her stomach;

her thumb hooked the front of her open jacket. There it remained until Pade stopped moving.

Gater stepped beside Pade and rolled his eyes before facing the three strangers.

"Well, Mr. Smith," Pade said, "I'm pretty sure my partner hasn't guaranteed we'll take the job. So I don't know why you're talking like you've already hired us."

"You're correct. Mr. Emmett told us you two would have to discuss it. But as I showed him, I am certain you will take the job. It's in your best interest."

Gater cleared his throat. "They, uh… They've got… Well, you'll want to hear them out."

The hair stood on Pade's neck, and he looked hard at Alex or Kelly, whatever the woman's name was. She gave no response. He calculated the speed at which he would need to draw his pistol in order to beat the woman to hers. *Shit!*

Pade glared at the suit. "What's this about?"

"We like the service you provide."

"We're haulers. There are a lot of us. You're welcome to go find one. Elsewhere."

"Hmm. But few, maybe none, operate a vessel like the *Arden-Dale.* That's why we're here."

"Look, Mr. Stiff—"

"Smith."

"Sure. I don't have time for your games." Pade reached for the tool bag with one hand and the pocket opening in his coveralls with the other, hoping to see these uninvited guests out. Gater didn't move. The woman pulled her jacket back and wrapped her fingers around the black grip of a holstered pistol. She gripped Smith's collar with her left hand.

"Uh-uh!" she warned. Her eyes locked on Paden's hands.

Pade stood slowly, keeping his hands open and visible. "Slog off!"

The woman relaxed.

Smith cleared his throat. "This is a unique ship. Old. Almost a hundred. Am I right?"

"What do you want?" Pade asked.

"I've always thought this ship model looked like a hatch turtle. You know, like the ones they found on Jorden, that moon orbiting Weaver-3."

Turtle? Pade wondered what kind of soaked-loaf wimp of a man stood before him. Pade had always thought the ship looked like a large, armored drop ship or a troop carrier. Perhaps a tank. *A turtle? Really?*

"Flying turtles." Smith shook his head. "Not many old Georges-HGs still break atmo, let alone make runs outside their systems. Those still operating have removed their Heinlein Gravity systems. Apparently, the grav systems consumed too much energy, and then there was that nasty business about the suits causing ulcers and tumors." He tapped a polished brown shoe on the cargo bay floor. "But you still have yours. That says something. Like, perhaps you have another reason for maintaining that power core. I bet—"

"My partner told you to piss off," Gater sneered.

"We'll leave when you've taken the job." Smith smiled, genuine at first, then it grew smug and certain. "All the other prospects backed out on you, hmm? It's a shame how things dried up. Seems we're the only job you've got, gentlemen."

Pade looked at Gater, who replied with their signal for *I said nothing.*

Smith's business face returned. "Back to your ship, then. You see, we think you power something other than the gravity system.

That's why we want you to transport something for us. Transport it to the other side of the quadrant using the same effort you made with that unregistered job three months ago to the Delta Quadrant, and with the similar one eight months before that in the outer Alpha. In fact, you have a three-year history of 'off the record' long-distance transports, and I stress 'long distance.'"

Smith's assumptions about the ship's unique power use aside, how did the man know about their runs to the Alon37 and Meleph-Deep systems? Pade studied him, wondering how much the man truly knew, but Smith's game face was unreadable.

Pade feigned incredulity. "There are no fold gates in those systems. And you can check every carry-all's manifest. We weren't on any of them."

"I don't have time for your games either, Mr. Deckard."

Smith reached into his attaché case. Pade and Gater both tensed, prepared to attack or move, but Smith pulled a datapad from the case, not a weapon.

He handed it to Pade and continued. "We've been following your ship's activities for years. Go ahead, take a look at the files."

Pade selected the first file, which pulled up a three-dimensional map of the Meleph-Deep system. He zoomed in on a blinking dot until it was big enough to see his ship's fake transponder signal, identifying it as a scientific research vessel. The files that followed showed photos of the *Arden-Dale* on the surface of Ariat Prime; of him and Gater helping offload crates of weapons, shaking hands with a formerly wanted man who was now dead. There were other files and reports in that folder. Each detailed their activity in a particular system. The device showed two more folders of files on its screen. One for each of the past two years. Pade knew what would be in those. His blood chilled.

"Are you Fedlaw?" he asked.

"No," Smith said. "And as long as you take our job, the Federation Law Service need not find out about any of this." He reached out and retrieved the datapad from Pade. "The weapon shipment was not very humanitarian of you, but the medical supplies you recently snuck onto Charyd showed you two have a noble side."

A port worker, in his smudged and faded yellow-and-orange outfit, walked by under the watchful eye of the muscleman at the end of the ramp. Everyone waited until he had walked away.

"They paid. That's all that mattered," Pade muttered.

"But medicine? Why hire you?"

Pade looked Smith in the eye. For all the man's lack of physical presence, he had the stare of an apex predator: callous, cold. He wasn't going to back down.

Pade held the gaze. "Charitable organizations don't have the credits that companies do. They're forced to be more frugal. Buying almost expired or recently expired meds is one way to get more done with their funds. The medicines are still good, but the freight won't get past customs. They paid. We hauled."

Smith smirked. "You claim that job was for the money. My colleagues and I believe you took the job because you felt guilty over the arms shipment. You're soft."

Gater snarled. "Eat shit!"

"I'll stick with wagyu beef and Drelan caviar." Smith paused and looked long at both men. "Are you two related?"

"Ha! No," Pade laughed.

"What?" Gater roared. "Related to this idiot? No way."

Pade snapped his head around to glare at his partner, a touch hurt. Gater avoided his stare.

Smith took a moment longer to look at them before he continued. "Listen well, both of you: if you fail to accept this commission or to deliver the cargo, all the information gleaned from our investigation will be sent to the authorities. Do we understand each other?"

"Yeah," Pade said. "Gater and I understand you're an asshole."

"Your military file labels you as 'difficult,' but you're much more than that." Smith rubbed his brow and sighed. "They had you on the fast track at one point. Were you aware of that?"

Pade didn't reply.

"It's true. But I see now why they cut your career short. Be assured, Mr. Deckard, we hold all the cards. You will take this job."

Pade glanced at his partner and then Smith's two bodyguards. "You can threaten us all you want, but we're not working for free, and we're not discussing the price until you tell us the cargo and destination."

Smith held his case in front of himself with both hands. "You and your partner will haul a crate and three passengers and never speak of the trip to anyone. We'll provide the destination once your ship clears Varen-4's rings. We've already transferred twenty thousand credits to your account, and another thirty will be yours once the cargo is delivered. Fifty thousand for no more than four days' work."

"You're shitting us," Pade scoffed.

Gater pulled his arm up and typed furiously on his wrist datapad. Smith waited. Pade watched. A few seconds later, Gater's eyes widened. He reached over and showed Pade the display.

InterStar Financial
Acct #1138UD4L4266117
Recent Deposit: 20,000.00
Source: Empyrenetics Corp.

Pade had to stop himself from whistling.

"What if it goes longer?" Gater asked.

"It won't," Smith said.

Pade licked his lips. "If it does, we get ten thousand extra at the start of each new regg." He held Smith's stare. The cargo bay grew quiet. Outside, the air handlers hummed, and the port's wheeled loaders whirred by.

"Fine," Smith said. "If it goes over four reggs, an extra ten thousand."

"Per regulated day. At the start of each regg-day."

"Agreed."

Gater turned to Pade. "What if they don't pay?"

Pade's eyes remained on Smith and narrowed. "They never see their cargo again."

Smith's jaw set. He glared at Pade. "The Fedlaw will be the least of your worries if you cross us, Mr. Deckard. You'll do well to remember that."

Pade sneered. "Based on what your corporation is willing to pay us to move this crate through untraceable channels, it must be worth a lot more than fifty K. Don't mess with *us*, Mr. Smith." He pointed a finger at the shorter man. "You'll get your delivery as long as you pay your fare. I promise you that."

"We'll hold you to that promise."

Pade knew there would be strings. Complications. There always were. He looked at the three strangers.

"You, the charm twins, and a crate?" Pade asked.

The woman stared. The man, without turning around, raised a middle finger to Pade. Pade knew the man wouldn't see it, but he smiled and waved back.

Smith shook his head. "No, Mr. Deckard. I will not be joining you."

What Pade had expected to arrive was something that would have taken no more than three or four people, perhaps a bot or two, to carry up the *Arden-Dale*'s cargo ramp. Smith's crate arrived on the bed of a commercial ground hauler and was, in fact, a shipping container. The kind one sees transported across the land on mag-rails or in convoys along roadways. This one was accompanied by two suits, three scientist-types, and a half dozen laborers.

Pade and Gater stared in disbelief from the catwalk that circled above the bay's floor. Smith lurked below.

"What the..." Pade fumed. "That's not a... a... a—"

Gater shook his head. "That's not a crate."

"That's not a crate!" Pade finished.

"Dayta, data," Smith said, swiping pages on his datapad.

Pade pointed at the container. "How much does that thing weigh?"

"It's within your ship's safe transport limit."

Gater continued to stare. "That's not a crate."

Smith looked up. "You're being paid well. You should have known it was going to be a special job. If anyone could do this, we'd have bid it out. Do you think we'd pay you the windfall you're getting otherwise?"

Pade didn't like it when others made sense. He couldn't argue against them.

He was about to climb down to help load the cargo when one of the laborers called up to him, "What system you got?"

"It's a Warn EXR."

"First series?"

Pade was impressed. "No. It's upgraded and has the Torque-Limiter package."

"Nice," the man said. "I got this." He shooed Pade with his hands and began to issue orders to the others around him.

One of the scientist-types did not appear to be so easily convinced of the man's confidence and inserted herself in the middle of the workers. The laborers smiled or showed no emotion when she looked their way, but rolled their eyes and shook their heads when her attention was drawn elsewhere.

It took longer than Pade had expected, but ultimately, they managed to line up the shipping container with the cargo bay's extended platform and secure it to the conveyor system. The metal container creaked and popped as it was pulled into the center of the bay. When it stopped, steel clamps seized the bottom with a loud bang, locking it to the floor. The laborers wasted no time having the delivery signed off and leaving as though they were missing the call for dinner.

Gater stared at the container, shaking his head. "This is why I don't like people." He turned and left the bay through the personnel airlock, heading into the main section of the ship.

"You and me both," Pade muttered.

The beige container bore no placards. No numbers. No company name. Brown primer paint coated what looked like recent patch repairs. The corrugated walls and roof displayed a few dents, but none were deep, and the paint had not been rubbed off or scraped. It all gave Pade the impression of being staged.

He slid down the ladder to the bay's floor. Scientists with handheld scanners and other instruments walked around the metal monstrosity, pausing occasionally, consulting their screens. They conferred and kept to themselves, ceasing their activities whenever Pade drew near, resuming only after he stepped away.

Pade rubbed his left knee and walked to the back, where the doors would be if it were a proper shipping container. He paused after rounding the corner. The woman scientist he'd seen among the laborers was there. Now that he had a good view of her, she was positively alluring. Her bronze skin glowed in the sunlight shining through the open cargo door, and her long, black hair whipped and tugged with the occasional breeze. She wore brown slacks, a white shirt, and sensible shoes, but made it all look charming.

She waited, dividing her attention between a handheld datapad and a Sapien Series-605 droid making its way onto the ship. The bipedal droid pulled a full-sized, wheeled power cube behind it, the kind that would take a loader, or four people working together, to push into place.

"Once you have the cube plugged in," she called to the droid, "make sure the subject is still sleeping and then run a scan. Verify it wasn't hurt during transport."

Subject? Pade didn't like the sound of that.

The droid replied with a polite woman's voice. "Yes, Dr. Odom." The white light making up its cylindrical head pulsed softly with each syllable. Although the 605's body was shaped like an average human, the metal skin covered only its servos and actuators, leaving its joints exposed, and it was not painted to look human. The head atop the torso allowed for three-sixty camera coverage around it, which typically differentiated utility droids from personal ones.

"And Dearie," Odom said, "run a diagnostic on yourself as well. I want us to be fully operational. Right?"

"Yes, Dr. Odom." The droid finished wheeling the power cube to the back of the container, placing it beside a personnel door built into the back wall. It began to install the cube.

Odom turned, almost running into Pade. Her brown eyes met his. He ran a hand through his sandy hair.

"Hey," he said with a smile.

Her eyes sparkled. Her lips parted.

"You're in my way," she said, her tone all business.

Pade moved aside, and she pushed past him. There was nothing warm or playful in it, and he thought he sensed disgust in her mannerisms. He wondered if he should have shaved. Then he discounted it. Maybe it was this planet. Did they have different customs on Varen-4? He'd never heard of such a thing, but it could be possible. After all, it couldn't be his looks.

In a matter of minutes, Smith had shaken hands with Dr. Odom, and he and the remaining scientists made their way off the ship, leaving behind Odom, the 605, and Alex and Kelly. The latter two checked several locked boxes, the kind that Pade, and any reasonable person, would properly call "crates."

The male closed a box and called out to the other one. "Alex, did they approve the Mark-30s?"

"Yeah," she said. "That box. Six mags each."

"APE?"

"Roger that."

That sorts them out, Pade thought. *The chick's Alex.* He wondered why she and Kelly, the crayon-muncher, needed that kind of firepower.

"Hey," he called to them. "Do I need to explain to you the dangers of using armor-piercing explosive rounds while we're off-planet?"

"Relax, mush boy," Alex said. "Just go sit down and fly this piece of junk." She pointed to the personnel door leading to the rest of the ship.

"You do your job," Kelly added. "Leave us to ours. If things go bad, you'll want us to have those M-30s."

Pade's blood rose. "If things go bad"? What kind of shit did we get into?

"There better not be that kind of trouble!" he said.

Gater's tinny voice came over the speaker system. "*Pade. Control has us in the launch queue.*"

"Better run along, mush boy," Alex mocked.

Pade pointed at them. "I'm serious."

Kelly moved his hand like a sock puppet chattering. *Piece of junk? Mush boy? I'll frickin' jettison your asses!*

Gritting his teeth, Pade keyed the intercom and replied to Gater, "On my way."

He walked to the bay's suit locker, hoping to grab a set of used and smelly Heinlein Grav Suits for the congeniality twins, but Gater had already laundered them all. Pade settled for suits that would be just small or large enough to be annoying. He threw them at the feet of Alex and Kelly.

"Put these on," he said, "unless you want to find yourself floating around this place. Your choice. I don't care either way."

Alex picked one up and looked it over. Made of a fire-retardant cloth and about as thin as a set of thermal underclothes, the suits had initially been black, but had faded to gray through their years of use. Glints of the metal woven into them shined here and there. The alloy threads interacted with the ship's grav-plating, giving the wearer a sense of gravity as it tugged on the suit. It was worn against the skin, used with the gloves and balaclava for the best effect. Most passengers simply wore the one-piece suit, though, which was sound practice—wearing the complete ensemble for too long led to nasty medical complications.

Alex frowned. "I thought these things caused tumors."

"Only if you haven't had the vaccine," Pade lied. He snapped his fingers. "Damn. I forgot. They don't give that out anymore. Too bad."

Alex scowled and gave Pade her middle finger.

He smiled at her and pointed at the third suit. "That one's for Doctor Full-of-Herself. I'll assume your droid is equipped with electro-mag feet. No suits for droids."

Alex and Kelly stared, but did not reply. Pade read the hate in their scowls. Seeing his work was done, and with a measure of self-satisfaction, he punched the button to close the cargo doors, exited the bay, and headed to the cockpit to join Gater.

Three hours later, they'd passed the rings of Varen-4 and were accelerating toward the dead outer planets. Pade and Gater always used the shadow of such planets to hide from sensor scans before activating their fold drive. They thought it helped them hide their activity, but Smith's presentation proved it didn't always work. Still, it was better than flaunting their small ship's unique ability, which was typically reserved for much larger craft and stationary fold gates run by the Federation.

The trip to the outer planets would take them a few hours. Another five minutes from that point would be needed to charge the Herullian Fold Drive, and seconds later, they would be at their passengers' coordinates.

After consulting the Varen system's space-time grav charts and adjusting their heading, Pade turned to Gater. "Hey, there's something in that container they call 'the subject.'"

"I don't like the sound of that. You don't think we're transporting a prisoner or something, do you?"

Pade shook his head. "No. Why would they need scientists for a prisoner?"

"Engineers."

"What?"

"Engineers," Gater repeated. "'Scientist' is only used in cheap holovids and old books."

"Whatever. It was the new passenger, the *scientist*, who called it 'the subject.'"

"Well, that new passenger, the *engineer*, looks cute. At least on the monitors."

Pade checked the status of the engines. "Yeah, she's easy on the eyes, but that cargo container has more personality than her."

Gater laughed and pointed at Pade. "Turned you down, did she?"

"No."

"Yes."

"Shut your loaf-hole, dipshit," Pade spat. "I never got time to talk to her."

"The old Pade wouldn't have needed her to give him time."

Gater had always been jealous of his way with the ladies. The few times Pade had failed to bed one, or so much as secure a comm ID link, had been like holidays for Gater. The engineer was practically giddy at his current failure.

"Well, you go talk to her, if you think you can."

"Maybe I will."

Pade waggled his head. "Maybe you won't."

Gater looked at the monitor showing the cargo bay again. He zoomed in on Odom and the 605. Pade cursed under his breath. Even through the monitor, Odom's beauty was apparent. Gater drummed his fingers on the control panel, then unbuckled himself from his flight chair.

"Sit back down," Pade said. "You're not going down there."

"Yes, I am."

"You'll only embarrass yourself."

"You sound worried."

Pade rolled his eyes.

"What's her name?"

"Dr. Odom."

Gater laughed again. "Really? You didn't even get a first name?"

He ducked out the open cockpit doorway just as Pade threw a flight glove at him. It bounced off the wall and lingered in the zero gravity, tumbling.

"Try opening with your fold drive conversion formula," Pade yelled after him. "That one always gets the ladies." He added quietly, with a smirk, "Gets them to fall asleep."

Although Pade had known where the Herullian Fold Drive was and how to get it, it was Gater's genius and experience working on Federation fold gates that had determined they could modify a Georges-HG's power core to power it. Further, it was his brilliance that had converted their ship's power to the eight-phase system the alien technology required. Those events and their calculations were Gater's go-to whenever he got nervous around a pretty lady. Math and science were his warm blankets and comfort food; occasionally, they were his wingman, and they failed in that post every time.

Pade watched the monitor and waited for Gater to enter the cargo bay. He did so like a teenager at his first dance, milling about by the wall and pretending to be interested in everything but Dr. Odom. Alex and Kelly watched him meander in, but stopped paying attention after the first few seconds. Odom sat on a crate next to the container and appeared to be reviewing something on her datapad.

The intercoms were beside each door, and when Gater neared one, Pade keyed the system. "Get back up here before you make a fool of yourself."

Gater looked into the camera, gave Pade both middle fingers, and mouthed the command for emphasis. He turned, raised his head, and strode toward Odom. With each step, his shoulders slouched until he eventually looked as nervous as he had when he'd entered the bay. He almost turned back, but she looked up and said something to him. They were too far from the intercom for Pade to hear their conversation, but he zoomed in for a better look.

Odom had to be wearing her grav suit, as she wasn't floating about the bay, but she'd left the balaclava off. Even with her hair pulled back in a tight ponytail, it was as mesmerizing as it had been while down around her shoulders, and her face was even more captivating than before. A strand of hair near her temple had avoided capture. It floated and teased.

She set the pad into a sleeve attached to her crate and stood, offering her hand, which Gater shook. What they spoke about for the next few seconds, Pade had no clue. Odom smiled a little and seemed genuinely interested in what Gater had to say. Gater's hands awkwardly searched for and found his pockets, he shuffled his feet, and his head bobbed here and there.

"Oh, God," Pade said to the empty cockpit. "He's getting nervous."

Gater's body swayed, and he rocked on his heels.

"No," Pade shouted at the monitor. "Don't do it."

Gater smiled and nodded fervently to something she had said, and his hands came out of his pockets. They began to gesture and move in that way Pade knew was Gater's story of how he'd come up with the conversion formula for their fold drive. Pade waited for Odom to yawn. For her to feign a need to return to work. For her to call the cockblock twins over to carry Gater away.

But Odom smiled and leaned in. She snared her floating black tress and tucked it behind her ear. She trailed her fingers along the length of her neck. She laughed. She reached out and touched Gater's arm.

"Son of a bitch!" Pade shut off the monitor.

Thirty minutes later, Gater glided into the cockpit, an unconscious smile adorning his face. He seemed light, as though his Heinlein Suit's connection with the deck plates were malfunctioning, but Pade knew better.

"Her name is Katie," he hummed. "The dragon's her project. She started with it during her internship."

"Dragon?" Pade asked.

"That's what the doltish duo call it."

"They're transporting a dragon? A real dragon? A living creature?"

"That's what I heard."

"There's no such thing. We'd have heard if an alien species like that had been encountered."

Gater snapped his fingers and pointed at Pade. "Well, there's at least one. And it's on our ship. And Katie's in charge of the project."

"Right," Pade sniped. Gater's joviality was driving him crazy.

"She got her PhD at K.T.I."

"That's nice."

"K-T-I, Pade. *The* Kaku Technology Institute."

"Yeah. So you said."

"She did her dissertation on Young's Variant."

"Uh-huh."

"She used my work to support it."

"Uh-huh."

"My articles. My work."

"Yeah." Pade needed to change the subject. He could tell Gater was getting on a roll, and the whole thing was only pissing him off. "Hey, uh, run the patch bots through a wake-up and diagnostic."

"Sure."

Pade had expected him to ask why that was needed. They always ran a diagnostic on the patch-and-repair robots before launch and never checked again until after they'd folded space. Yet Gater started activating the system, hitting buttons and tapping the monitor.

"Boop," he said with each tap, smiling the whole time. "Boop."

"A little more focus, please."

"Don't worry about me. I'm operating at one hundred percent. Boop. By the way, she holds the same belief I do on Exchange Theory."

She had to be a nerd. "Great."

"Patch-and-repair bots are fully operational. Fleet compliment at ninety-one-point-six, six percent." Gater glanced at Pade and stated what they both knew too well. "One bot is still down."

"Thanks."

Gater closed the screen with a loud, "Boop! Maybe you should run a diagnostic on yourself. I think you're running a little jealous."

Pade laughed, perhaps too forcefully. "Jealous? Me?"

Alex cleared her throat.

Pade and Gater turned to find her standing in the cockpit's entryway, shaking her head. "Are you done acting like children? How about you at least pretend you're grown up?" She shook her head. "I've received comms from the planet. A Celestial Class ship has changed heading and is now running a bearing parallel to ours."

Gater swung in his chair and worked his monitor. "I got it. One-point-one-four terameters. One-six-eight degrees to our heading. Negative four degrees zed. It's matching our velocity."

"What kind of illegal shit are we hauling?" Pade snapped at Alex.

"I can't tell if they've launched any smaller craft," Gater continued. "They're using Varen-6 like we are, trying to hide their movement. Should I perform an active scan?"

"No!" Pade and Alex said together.

Pade turned to his partner. "That'll let them know we're onto them, and if we're hidden from them now, it'll only give away our position."

"They could have snuck up on us," Alex said. "You two are worthless."

"Why is Fedlaw after us?" Pade asked.

"It isn't the Law Service." Her wristpad beeped, and she glanced at it.

"The military?" Pade asked in disbelief.

"It has no Federation identifier, Pade," Gater said, looking at his screen. "It's privately owned."

"What?" Pade asked. "Who can afford a Celestial Class ship?"

Alex looked up from her device. "Our competitors. I can't believe Smith trusted you with this mission. This is corporate warfare, boys. They want what's in the crate, and if they can't get it, they'll kill the entire project."

"The dragon?" Gater asked.

Alex opened her mouth, but seemed to catch herself before saying anything. She turned and left the cockpit, heading back to the cargo hold. "Get us to those coordinates laser-fast," she called out from the corridor. "For all of our sakes."

"I've got ghost images popping in and out," Gater said, his eyes fixed on the monitor. "Two light craft. Fast movers. Closest is point-nine terameters. They're closing." He looked up. "They wouldn't shoot at us, would they?"

"I don't want to find out," Pade replied.

"How far are we from the selected fold point?"

"Just over two hours."

Gater's fingers danced and flew over his control board and monitors. "Based on their closing speeds, if they intend to engage, we have less than half an hour before they're close enough. If they carry missiles, you can cut that time to minutes."

"Do some of that math shit. Get us a closer fold point."

"Already started the calculations. The destination isn't changing. That saves us a lot of time. Nav computer will have a solution for a point on our current trajectory in fifteen minutes." He flipped a toggle and pointed at Pade.

"Got it. Fold point locked in. Countdown started."

Pade reached back to pull his restraint harness around himself. He locked the buckle and keyed the intercom system.

"Listen up," he said over the old speakers. "The situation has evolved. We will be making the fold in less than fifteen minutes. Gravity will be disabled in nine and a half minutes. So, lock down your gear, find a seat, and buckle up. That is, unless you want to find yourself bouncing around the cargo area like a rubber ball. Pade out."

"Computations looking good so far." Gater belted himself into his seat.

"I'll start a last diagnostic on the folder while you finish that." Pade pulled up the device on his monitor and went through the sequence.

A voice crackled through the intercom system, and a beautiful but concerned face appeared on the screen in the cockpit. "Captain Pade? Captain Pade?" Odom's voice was urgent. The 605 stood behind her.

Pade looked at Gater. "Captain Pade. I like that."

"Captain Pade? This is Dr. Odom. Can you hear me?"

Pade keyed the system. "This is Captain Pade. We're pretty busy up here."

"Be nice," Gater whispered.

"Captain Pade, you can't just change the fold time."

"Yes, I can. And I just did. Secure your gear and see to your... your crate."

"Oh dear," the 605 said, lights pulsing.

"No—I mean, I need more time."

"You have enough time," Pade said.

"We did." Odom paused. "We were on path before you changed it. The project needs prep time before we fold space."

"You have time. Fifteen minutes."

Gater slapped Pade's arm. "I told you to be nice."

"Fifteen minutes is not enough. The buffers take an hour to install. We don't know how the system will react without the precautions in place. The folding may shock it."

"We don't have an hour," Pade shrugged. "But tell you what, if you want more time, we can dump you and your crate off this ship, and you can ask the folks in that big-ass ship and the two bogeys closing in on us if they'll give it to you. This ship has fifteen minutes. Correction, twelve minutes and eight seconds. Out." He turned off his comm monitor.

A minute later, Dr. Odom shot through the cockpit door with a look of loathing. Pade and Gater turned in their chairs to face her. She wagged her finger at Pade, lips pursed, nose flaring, and he wasn't sure if she was too angry to speak or trying to catch her breath.

"Hey, Katie," Gater said.

Odom smiled at him, her eyes lighting up. "Hi." Then her look turned serious. "This is between me and your brother."

"You told her we were brothers? Why would you do that?"

"Well... I—" Gater started.

"Do you know how much time I've devoted to this project?" Odom interrupted.

"That doesn't matter," Pade said.

"I've given my life to it."

The 605's voice came across Odom's comm device. "Oh dear. Dr. Odom?"

"What is it now?" she asked.

"Mr. Kelly entered the mobile lab looking for you," the 605 said. "He knocked the heat capture hood loose."

Odom looked perplexed. "How did he manage that?"

The 605 continued. "He's trying to replace it, but can't get the straps back over the head."

Odom's eyes popped wide. She paled. "Oh, God. He'll get burned alive if the subject wakes up. On my way." She bolted from the cockpit.

"Should we be worried?" Gater asked Pade.

"Maybe, but there's nothing we can do about it. We're caught between the devil and the cold black void."

Gater glanced between the sensor readings of the approaching ships and the video feed of the cargo bay. He nodded. "Yeah." Then he added, "I told you it was a dragon."

"You're a dumbass. There's no such thing."

Minutes rolled by. The video display showed Odom moving in and out of the shipping container, instruments in hand. The 605 remained inside. Kelly, who Odom had escorted, unhappy but un-singed, from the container, worked to secure his gear. Alex assisted, animated and apparently giving Kelly an earful of something un-pleasant.

With the two approaching light craft and the one massive ship shadowing them, Pade and Gater focused their attention between their pursuers and the approaching fold point. The video monitor was locked into displaying charts and the approach vector.

"Six minutes," Gater stated.

"I see it. I see it." Pade keyed the intercom's speakers. "One minute 'til zero G, folks. One minute to lock your ass into a seat."

A few seconds later, Odom's voice came across the intercom. "Captain Pade, I need more time! Can't you give me fifteen, even ten more minutes?"

"We're pushing it with the approaching craft already."

Pade looked at his engineer. Gater consulted his screen and nodded.

"And," Pade continued, "if we change the time, we'll need to run all new calculations for the new fold point."

"But—" she started.

"Look! We're not going through a Federation fold gate. We can't simply park outside while you prepare your special project and have a cup of tea. I have no time for this. We're done." Pade shut off power to the intercom system.

"Forty-five seconds," Gater said.

"I see it."

They worked their controls. The intercom beeped. "Really, Captain?" Odom said. "You think powering the comms down will stop me?"

Pade shut the system down again without a word and locked its controls. He and Gater continued to run through their pre-fold checklist.

Seconds later, the comms beeped again, and Odom's face glared at him from his screen. The 605 stood behind her.

"What do I have to do," she asked, "hit you in the head with a hammer? I have several advanced engineering degrees, Captain. Did you really think you could silence me?"

Pade reached for the grav system's control switch and lifted the protective cover.

"Captain!" Odom spat.

"You're early," Gater said.

"I don't care." Pade flipped the gravity switch, disabling the system.

"Cap—"

Fury was replaced by shock as Odom suddenly looked off-balance.

"Oh dear," the 605 stated, reaching out to steady the doctor.

Pade turned the intercom off again. "Start charging the drive."

"Already done. Drive is on auto." Gater looked at his monitor. "Five minutes."

"Approach is steady. We are go."

Three minutes passed before they heard grunting and banging from the corridor outside. Both men turned and watched a floating Odom pulling herself along the conduits and metal beams of the ship, navigating her way into the cockpit. Her bronze face glistened from the exertion. Dark hairs had pulled free of her ponytail and stood wild from her head. She was no less beautiful.

"You son of a bitch!" she shouted.

Gater turned back to his console, silent.

There were two extra chairs in the cockpit, and Pade pointed to one. "Better get yourself locked into that seat, doc." He turned back to his console as she grabbed the headrest.

"You have to stop the countdown," she grunted, pulling herself into the seat and positioning her harness. "We've never put the subject through a test like this."

Pade looked at Gater mockingly. "Problems with the *dragon?*"

"Possibly? How do you know… Never mind. I prefer 'subject.' Calling it 'dragon' is too purposeful. It lacks complexity, uniqueness."

Gater smiled at Pade. "You called it a dragon."

"I was mocking you," Pade said. "Couldn't you feel the sarcasm?"

"Seriously," Odom said. "Stop the fold."

"Can't," Pade said.

Clearly frustrated, Odom turned to Gater.

He ducked his head and spun in his seat to face the console. "Fifty seconds."

"Engines are shut down," Pade said.

Odom grew visibly more concerned. "Young's Variant. I don't know how it will affect the subject."

"Thirty seconds to fold," Pade announced over the intercom.

"Gater," Odom pleaded, "tell this fool the dangers of Young's Variant."

"Please, Doctor Odom," Pade said. "Even I know Young's Variant applies to energy transfer between points in space-time. It doesn't apply to biological tissue."

"What?" Odom asked.

Gater looked at the monitor. "Five seconds."

"Oh, shit!" Odom fumbled with her harness buckle.

It clicked.

The console lights faded.

The stars outside the windows shifted and blurred.

The ship shuddered.

Both men looked around the cockpit. Together they said, "That's not right."

The console lit back up.

The stars cleared and shined bright again, but drifted by the window, right to left.

An orange light flashed above the cockpit exit, and a warning buzzer toned. *"Warning. Subspace pulse detected,"* a woman's voice stated.

"We're listing," Pade said. "No, we're tumbling."

"Oh, shit," Odom said again.

"Warning. Subspace pulse detected," the voice repeated.

"We've fold-shifted," Gater said, tapping his screen.

"Warning. Subspace pulse detected."

"Stabilizers are firing," Pade said. "Tumble slowing."

"Where are we?" Gater asked.

Pade moved between screens. "Computer hasn't found us yet."

"Warning."

The cockpit dimmed.

"Power core shutdown in progress."

"Ah, crap," Pade said.

Gater conferred with his monitor. "Power core overheated. It's in shutdown."

"Yeah," Pade said. "I heard that. Tumble slowed, but stabilizers are now offline."

"Warning. Power core shutdown in progress."

The 605's voice came across Odom's comm device. "Dr. Odom."

"Nav computer's down too," Pade said.

Odom spoke into the device. "We're kind of busy, Dearie."

"We may have an issue. The subject appears to be waking up."

Wide-eyed, Odom gasped.

"Warning. Power core shutdown in progress."

"Oh my God!" she said.

"Dr. Odom, how should I pro—oh dear—" There was a loud screech, like the sound of rending metal. The comm went silent. The cockpit darkened, lit only by a few dim emergency lights.

There were no more warnings.

The hum of the air handlers stopped.

The steady pulse of the cooling pumps and the random ticks and beeps all ended. Pade swore he felt the temperature drop, like cold fingers running over his body, grabbing the back of his neck.

Gater's voice broke the eerie quiet. "Auxiliary power should come on in a sec."

A large bang emanated from deep in the ship, and Pade felt the cockpit's panels vibrate, jolting the three occupants. They looked at each other. Several smaller bangs and a staccato, almost buzzing sound followed.

"I've gotta get down there," Odom said.

Two warning tones preceded the computer's next announcement. "*Auxiliary power online.*"

The control panel lit up, and the lighting and noise returned to normal inside the cockpit. Pade breathed a sigh of relief, and he and Gater worked their controls, fingers tapping and bounding. Odom unbuckled her belt.

"I'd advise against that just now," Pade said.

"Auxiliary doesn't activate the flooring," Gater added. "No gravity." His foot tapped the flooring absentmindedly.

"I have to get down there." Concern held her face hostage as she waited.

It took several minutes for Gater to get the monitors online and the cameras linked. Pade worked on bringing the nav computers up to speed and discovering the ship's coordinates.

Gater gave his screen a definitive poke with his index finger. "Systems online."

"Warning. Hull breach in primary cargo bay."

"Shit," Pade said. "Activating patch bots."

"Warning. Possible fire in primary cargo bay."

"Warning. Power drain from conduit P-2. Systems affected: Sensor arrays. Life support. Water recyclers—"

Odom fidgeted.

Pade looked at Gater. "Shut that thing off."

"Waste management—"

Gater worked his controls, and the computer ceased its announcements. The last did not sit well with them. They both knew the P-2 conduit ran just beneath the catwalk in the cargo bay and powered some of the ship's essential systems.

Pade leaned closer to Gater and whispered, "Does auxiliary power use conduit P-2?"

"No," Gater whispered back. "But primary does."

Pade knew they'd have to fix it along with the damaged cables inside if they wanted to count their future in years instead of hours.

The computer dinged. Pade read his screen. "Nav has us placed in Zone Two, outer Beta Quadrant."

"We're way off course," Odom said.

Pade continued. "Sector Oscar-Three. Nearest inhabited system, Childsbreath, is nineteen-point-eight light years away. Sending distress signal." He lifted a cover and flipped a switch.

"Subspace transmitter offline."

He toggled the switch again.

"Subspace transmitter offline."

"Shit!"

"Radio transmitter is operational," Gater said.

"Great," Pade sneered. "We can expect help in a couple of decades, if we're lucky."

"It's better than nothing at this point," Odom offered. "We don't even know who's out here. There could be a ship nearby."

Pade put his headset on and recorded a distress message. He sent it out on a wideband broadcast.

"I've got the cameras up," Gater said.

Pade and Odom carefully got up from their seats, holding tightly to Gater's chair. Pade wedged his feet under the control console to lock himself down. Odom hovered at an angle, her head next to Gater's as she watched the screen.

Gater pulled up the cargo bay. The monitor showed a hazy scene. Particles hung in the foggy air. Frost covered everything. The shipping container sat as it had, but the personnel door was open. Yellow strobe lights blinked, giving their warning to evacuate. The light glistened off flecks of ice crystals inside the bay. Nothing moved beyond some small, floating debris.

Gater switched to a second camera, one with a view of the back of the container and a small portion of its interior through the open personnel door. The inside was dark, but lights flickered randomly within. In the moments that flashes gave them a glimpse, they saw papers, a few datapads—and a forearm and hand detached from its body. The limb, pale and icy, hovered in the entrance.

"Oh, God," Odom said. "Uh... I think that's Alex."

Pade nodded somberly.

Gater asked, "Where's Kelly?"

He switched cameras again, and everyone jolted.

Kelly's body floated by, spinning slowly. It turned, the face staring into the camera, pale with dark blotches, an open mouth, and dull, frosted eyes. The corpse had found its way close to the catwalk that ran around the bay, ten feet above floor level.

Pade pointed at the holes that perforated the front of Kelly's jacket—there were at least seven. "Looks like he's been shot."

Odom's wide eyes filled with sadness, her hand over her mouth. She shook her head.

"Did he attack Alex? Did she turn on him?" Gater asked.

"Crap. Bullets probably caused the hull breaches," Pade said. "We should know soon enough. The patch bots can fix those."

"But why would Alex shoot Kelly?" Gater asked.

"Uh," Odom said, hesitation in her voice. "I think it was my subject."

"What?" Pade snapped. "You had a person in there?"

"No!" she shouted in frustration.

"Dragon," Gater offered.

Pade stared at him incredulously. "A gun-wielding dragon? Really, Gater?"

"That isn't far from the truth," Odom said. She worked on her wrist datapad, tapping and dragging.

Pade stared at Odom. "What the hell!"

Gater continued to check the camera feeds.

"Damn!" Odom finally said. "Our link's disconnected."

"What link?" Pade snapped. "Start telling us the truth, damnit!"

"Hey," Gater said, eyes on the monitor.

Pade ignored him. "What are you not telling us?"

"Guys," Gater said.

Odom continued to work on the datapad.

"What the hell is going on, doc?" Pade demanded.

"I can't reach Dearie either," Odom said.

"Hey, guys," Gater said. "What's that?"

They turned to see him pointing at the monitor. There, in an area cloaked in shadow that even the yellow strobe did not penetrate, was movement.

Two red ovals glowed within the gloom.

"What the hell is that?" Pade yelled.

"The dragon," Gater said.

"Alright," Odom sighed, "since you insist on being crude... Yes. That looks like the DRAGAN."

Pade almost lost his grip on Gater's chair. "What?"

"It's one of our military projects. They call it the Droid for Reconnaissance And Ground Asset Neutralization. DRAGAN, or more simply, the dragon. We were headed to a testing site."

"A droid?" Gater asked.

"An armed, untested droid?" Pade added.

Odom looked hurt. "It doesn't have all its weaponry and tools at this time. The only weapons it can use are the head's supplemented heat discharge and the coaxial short-barrel weapon. That weapon has to be loaded before the power source is installed. I don't understand it, though. Several safeties are in place to prevent it from arming. But don't worry—it's empty now. It's designed to dump the full magazine, twelve rounds, all at once."

Pade was not convinced. "You said something about other weapons?"

"Uh, yes, but the light cannon, rockets, and explosive devices are not loaded until the subject is in final preparation for deployment." She returned to her datapad.

"Rockets?" Gater asked excitedly. "Really?"

"Wait," Pade said. "That thing carries explosives?"

"Various munitions, mines, and protective measures," Odom said, tapping her screen. "They're not loaded now."

"But you brought explosives onto my ship!" Pade said.

"Our ship," Gater corrected, "and I'm sure they're stored safely. Right, Katie?"

"Absolutely."

Pade shook his head and threw Gater a nasty look. "Well, how do we stop it? Please tell me you've got some kind of override on that wristpad of yours."

"Yeah, about that," Odom said, eyes on her datapad. "I do, but I can't seem to link with the subject at this time, and according to my readings, it may be operating in preservation mode. Which could explain the safeties failing on the coaxial weapon. I'm trying to find out why."

"What?" Pade asked.

Odom tapped and swiped. "That's not right."

"What?" Pade repeated.

"I'm totally locked out now," Odom said.

"You gotta be kidding me," Pade spat.

Odom stopped her work and pointed to the monitor showing the cargo bay. "We need to get in there."

On the screen, the eyes stared from the darkness.

"There? With the killer droid?" Pade said. "Right."

"Why?" Gater asked. "Why do you need to get in there?"

"There's an emergency shutdown device in the mobile lab," she said. "It may shut the subject off."

"May?" Pade and Gater asked together.

"Okay, will. It will."

"Are you sure?" Pade asked.

Odom hesitated.

"Oh, hell no," Pade said. "We're not going in there." He turned toward his console, pulling up the status on the patch bots. Gater turned to the monitor, moving the video relay to the screen above the cockpit's windows and running diagnostics on the ship's systems.

"Gater," Odom pleaded. "We need to get in there. I know we can shut off the subject remotely."

He turned to her, his eyes and hands pleading for patience. "Let us get primary power online, and then we'll figure out how to secure that thing. Anyway, it's contained now." He turned toward Pade. "Right?"

Pade ignored him. "Eight six-millimeter breaches in the hull located. Patch bots have repaired seven. Working on last one now. I'll send the others to check the damaged power cable."

"You'll go in after power's restored?" Odom asked. "Right?"

"Oh," Pade said. "Now it's us, not you?"

"Well, I work in a lab. I'm not trained for... for that kind of thing."

Two rapid buzzes sounded from the console. Pade turned, knowing the news was not good. "Bot One down. Last indicator had it at P-2 conduit. Number Nine is almost there."

Two more buzzes.

"What's that mean?" Odom asked. She moved to hover over his shoulder. Gater leaned in.

Pade remained focused on his screens. "Nine's down. Both bots no longer transmitting. Ten's approaching the conduit. I'm pulling up its camera."

The screen showed a low-angled video shot from the bot's perspective. The small six-legged repair robot approached the metal wall. Two legs reached out, and it began climbing the wall and its latticework of structural beams and piping. A metal tube, no thicker than a person's forearm, came into focus and stretched out across the screen as the robot approached.

"That's P-2," Pade said.

The camera glitched, and the angle changed abruptly. The screen went dark.

Bzz-bzz.

"What the—" Gater said.

"Get a camera on that section and light it up," Pade ordered.

Gater's fingers tapped and danced. A few seconds later, the overhead screen flickered, revealing that section of the cargo bay and its secret.

Pade growled.

Gater sighed. "Oh, shit."

Odom's eyes shot wide. "Oh, dear."

The dragon had wedged itself into a spot between the P-2 conduit and the bottom of the catwalk's grated flooring. The terror crouched atop the damaged tubing like a large panther protecting a kill. Mechanized muscles and a synthetic skeleton bulged and pressed against taut polymer skin. It was a dull gray, almost the size of a large hoverbike or one of Earth's lions. Its tail slithered and coiled and tightened around a nearby support beam. Its reptilian head twisted on a long neck, eyes scanning until they stared through the video screen at the three people in the cockpit. Beneath one of its clawed front feet was a mangled patch bot. Bits of metal floated and twisted nearby, glinting as they spun in zero gravity.

The dragon opened its mouth, revealing a dark opening where the throat would be. A glow emanated from within the darkness.

Odom's fingers clenched onto Gater's headrest. "Uh-oh."

Heat distortion warped the camera's view. A *No Signal* notice on a black screen replaced the picture the camera had shown seconds before.

Several lights blinked on the cockpit's control panel. "*Warning. Possible fire in primary cargo bay.*"

"What the hell!" Pade checked the various camera angles but couldn't find any flame or smoke.

"What are you not telling us, Katie?" Gater asked.

"Um," Odom said. "The subject—"

"You mean that damn dragon," Pade sniped.

"Hey," Gater protested.

"Yeah," Odom said. "The dragon. It can augment its heat venting system and discharge it in a concentrated blast. It's one of its defense options."

"On my ship?" Pade asked.

"Our ship," Gater said. "Why's it positioned above the conduit?"

"Are there heat exchangers inside it?" Odom asked.

Gater shook his head. "No, but there's a life support supply register behind the dragon. That has to be pumping out some heat now. Why?"

"The subject's not made to operate in the temperatures of space. The cold's probably causing power and mobility problems. It's trying to get warm, especially after it just vented that much heat. I doubt it'll do that again. Now's the perfect time to go in there and try the remote override."

Pade barked a humorless laugh. "That damn thing's killed two people. I'm not going to walk up and ask it nicely if we can repair *our* ship."

Gater glanced at Pade. "Thank you."

"It won't be dangerous once it's shut down."

"It dies," Pade said.

"You can't. You don't understand. It's the only working prototype—"

"I'm done listening, doc," Pade said. Gater's shoulders slumped in resignation.

121

"This program will save lives. It'll keep marines and soldiers from being ambushed."

Pade pointed at the screen. "Tell that to Alex and Kelly. It dies."

"No!" Odom worked her wrist datapad, tapping and swiping. Pade thought he saw tears welling in her eyes.

"What do you need from me?" Gater asked.

"We need to get power on and repair that conduit. Auxiliary gives us, what, six hours of life support?" Pade asked.

"Listen to me," Odom began, not looking up from her wrist.

"Closer to nine," Gater said, "if we shut down non-essential systems."

"The AI it uses is unique."

"Shut them down," Pade said, "and shut down life support in the bay. If it doesn't like the cold, let's ice the bitch. Then get down to the engine room and get the power core back online, but don't send power until you've heard from me that P-2's been fixed."

Odom placed her hand on Gater's arm, fingers pleading. "I've spent eight years on this program. I know I can shut it down."

Gater didn't acknowledge her. Instead, he tilted his head toward Pade as he worked his monitor and the switches on his console. "What are you going to do?"

Pade rubbed his top teeth over his bottom lip. "I think… Yeah. It's time to get—"

"Happy?" Gater asked.

Pade smiled. "Yeah."

Odom glanced between them, her brow scrunched in confusion. She looked back down at her pad and tapped it once more.

Gater chuckled and grabbed two comm devices from their slots under the console. He clipped one over his ear before handing the other to Pade. Gater unbuckled his restraints, turned, and launched himself from the back of his chair, making his way through the cockpit door and down the hallway with practiced accuracy. Pade placed his comm device over his ear, took one last look at the monitor, and unbuckled himself. He turned and grabbed Odom's wrist.

"Hey!" she snapped.

"You're coming with me," he said.

"Like hell I am."

"We can't afford to let anything happen to you. Besides, I'm not leaving you in here, Miss 'Several-Advanced-Degrees.'"

"That's *Doctor* 'Advanced-Degrees' to you," she sniped as he tugged her behind him. She tried to resist his efforts, latching on to what she could, but the zero gravity and Pade's strength and familiarity with the ship's handholds defeated her limited attempts.

It did not take long before Odom's need to protect herself from crashing into a beam or wall overrode her desire to struggle against Pade, and the two drifted almost as one as they negotiated the final corridor. They stopped outside the primer-white door to Pade's quarters, and he pulled her to his side, guiding her hand to a handle beside the portal.

"Grab that and wait here," he said, letting go and using his free hand to push the actuator button. The door popped inward with a soft clunk and slid into the wall with a hiss. Darkness met them, but lights flickered to life inside the room a moment later. Pade expected Odom to comment on the mess, but she didn't. She did, however, sneer in revulsion.

"Don't flatter yourself, Captain. You're not that charming."

Pade pushed himself into the room and floated to the back wall. "Please, doc. I'm not into your type."

"What? Sober?"

"No. Stuck-up and frigid."

"Asshole."

Pade smiled. He arrived at his weapon locker, bracing against the ceiling and wedging a foot under a bar on the floor as he entered the keypad's code. The locker's articulated door rolled away, revealing a host of magazines and boxes, four handguns, two rifles, and the smoothbore beauty he reserved for use onboard the ship whenever they were in flight. He smiled as he picked up the shotgun.

"What the hell?" Odom exclaimed. "What's that?"

"Happy," Pade said as he grabbed two magazines. The first was plain black and loaded with hull-safe shells. The other displayed a yellow stripe and was loaded with NED shells—neuro/electrical disruptors. He pocketed the first magazine.

"Happy? Really?" Odom asked, her face twisted in disgust.

Pade slapped the NED magazine into the receiver and pulled the charging handle to the rear. He smirked at Odom, releasing the handle and letting the weapon's bolt slam the first round into the chamber with a satisfying *clack*.

"Yeah," he said. "She makes me so happy."

"And I thought I'd feel guilty about this…"

Pade didn't like her tone or the look on her face. "What are you—"

She stared at him, shook her head, and muttered, "Hammer." Odom tapped her datapad, and the door to his room hissed closed, locking tight with a clunk and sealing him alone in his room.

Pade unwedged his foot and kicked off the wall, launching himself to the door. He slung Happy over his shoulder, pushed the door's actuator, and waited for the portal to open.

Nothing happened. He tried again, harder this time. Still nothing.

The room went dark.

"Lights on," he said. The darkness remained. "You gotta be kidding me."

This wasn't the first time he'd been locked in his quarters. Gater had done it to him once before. That time, in his seclusion, Pade had found a way to get by the override. He'd practiced it since then and could do it quickly. This time, with the dark and the lack of gravity, he'd be slowed down. Having Gater do it remotely would be much faster and much easier.

He tapped his comm device. The link to Gater opened, and a loud whirring and beeping from the engine room blared. "Yeah, Pade, what you need?" Gater shouted. He was barely audible over the blast of noise.

"Odom's loose," Pade shouted. "She's found a way to lock me in my quarters."

"A snooze in your quarters?" Gater shouted back. "Understood. But you coulda told me this later. I gotta get back to work."

"No! I need you to unlock—my—door!"

"Yeah. I agree. Leave it unlocked in case she needs to get out. Seriously, Pade, why you worried about getting my thoughts on it? I gotta get the power on, man." Gater closed the link, leaving only the hushed whir of the life support system in the quarters.

Pade became acutely aware of how much his knee ached. He screamed into the blackness, cursing the parents of a certain woman with several advanced degrees.

It's going to be the hard way after all.

Nine minutes and thirty-eight expletives later, he pushed his door to the side, and the light of the corridor crept into his room. Pade whipped off his headlamp and pocketed it with the multi-tool and powerpack he'd used to bypass the door's locks. He slung Happy once more and pulled himself into the hall, propelling from handhold to bar to beam with the agility he'd developed over the

125

many years he and Gater had flown the ship. Along the way, he thought of the joy it would bring him to drag Odom to the alternate cargo chamber and lock her in one of the empty containers there.

We'll let her out. Eventually. Maybe.

He pulled himself along the stairway to the airlock hatch for the cargo bay. Movement inside the airlock caught his attention, and he gazed through the thick window just in time to see Odom stepping through the open door into the bay. She had donned one of the ship's spacesuits and helmets. It was clear she had worked in a suit and mag-boots before, and she moved with an ease and fluidity few could achieve.

Odom turned to close the airlock door; her eyes locked with Pade's. In that glimpse, he saw the same expression he'd seen before in the eyes of new soldiers making their first orbital combat drop.

Odom turned away, and the door slid and locked into place.

Pade reached for the controls, ordering the first of the airlock's two doors to open. The orange light on the console flashed, and a twenty-second countdown started as the chamber rose to one atmosphere. He felt as though he could have read the entirety of the Intergalactic Shipping Conference's policy manual in the time the chamber took to regulate. Finally, the light turned green, and he slid through the door as soon as the opening was large enough. Happy screeched in protest as it ground against the durasteel frame.

Pade launched himself to the other door and looked through the window. A handful of crates and tools floated in the large cargo bay. Odom had just reached the floor and was moving to the back of the container. A few steps later, she disappeared from his view.

Pade pressed the side of his head against the glass, trying to glimpse the dragon. He knew where it had been, but the catwalk blocked his line of sight. He thought he saw its tail still wrapped around a beam, but the body wasn't visible.

He pushed away from the door, floated to his spacesuit's locker, and punched the code into the pad. The door slid open, revealing the suit and spare equipment. Pade grabbed the control pad on his suit's forearm and paired his comm device with the suit's system. He immediately opened the suit-to-suit channel and slid into it.

"What are you doing, doc?" he grunted into his mic.

There was no reply.

"Doc. Talk to me." Pade examined the open suit locker, the one Odom had used. All lights were green, and a NitroStall inhaler, its seal broken, lay atop a shelf.

Not her first jump.

"Doc. What are you thinking?"

Rapid, shallow breathing came through his speaker. "I can't let you destroy it." Her voice wavered and cracked. "Oh my God. Alex. Oh God."

"Don't look at the body."

"I have to move her to get to the crate."

"Doc. Listen. You're not going to help any of us getting yourself killed in there."

She took a breath. "The subject's in preservation mode. That's its reboot default. As long as I don't attack it, it won't come after me."

"It went after those patch bots."

"They must've gotten too close. I won't have to leave the lab. It'll never know what I'm doing—ah. Found it. I can deactivate it from in here."

Pade activated the mag-boots, finished securing the helmet, and thrust his hands into the locker's gloving slots, allowing the system to connect his gloves to the suit's sleeves.

"Powering the box up," Odom said.

"Wait. Wait. Let me get in there to help you—"

"No. You'll shoot my baby."

"Only if I have to. I promise. I'm trying to keep everyone alive." Pade felt his suit pressurize.

"Just stay up there. I've got this. Oh, shit!"

"What? Is it the dragon?"

"No. I can't establish a link in here."

She's gonna give me a heart attack.

"Must be the lab's walls. I have to step out."

"Wait," Pade pleaded. A green *GO* popped up on the bottom of the helmet's HUD, accompanied by the suit's system talking to him.

"All connections secure," it said. *"Power at ninety-nine percent."*

Pade clunked to the hatch and hit the airlock's control to open the inner door. The outer door shut, as expected, but nothing else happened. He looked down at the control panel and pushed the button again. The screen pulsed red once, but there was no other change.

"You're shitting me. This door too?" He cursed, forgetting the comms channel was open.

"I need you to stay up there."

"You're really pissing me off now."

"It'll be alright." Odom's shallow breathing said she didn't believe her own words.

Pade moved to the window again and watched her come into view on the other side of the shipping container. He strained, pushing the helmet against the window to see where the dragon was hiding, but its bulk prevented him from glimpsing anything, not even the dragon's tail.

He stepped back to his locker and grabbed Happy, pulling it to his shoulder to shoot the glass. A glimpse of yellow caught his attention, and he took a moment to check the magazine. A yellow stripe was wrapped around it.

NEDs! Damnit!

The other magazine sat in his jacket pocket, and he thought about reaching into the locker for it but stopped, remembering it was loaded with hull-safe shells. He could fire both magazines at the door or the window and still not get through. In fact, it would likely lead to frag flying around the inside of the airlock and puncturing his suit.

He gritted his teeth, kicked the door, and used his most profane curse.

"Captain!" Odom said. "Even I thought you were better than that."

He tried a different approach and spoke gently. "Katie, open this door."

"I'm sorry, Pade. I'm afraid I can't do that."

Pade slammed the butt of the gun into the permaglass. Nothing happened. His anger and frustration flared hotter. He looked back out the window. Carrying a keyboard-sized box, Odom was inching her way toward the broken conduit and the dragon.

"No signal," she said. "Moving closer. It's going to be okay."

"Don't do it," Pade pleaded. "Let me help."

"It's going to be okay," she said. Her voice was quiet, her breathing shallow and frenetic. "It's going to be okay," she repeated to herself.

Pade switched the commlink frequency, pulling up Gater's comm device. "Gater. Gater. I need you." He repeated the message as he tried the airlock controls one more time. Still no joy.

A loud whirring and Gater's voice shouting into his mic tore into Pade's ear. "What now?" he asked. "I'm in the middle of getting the primary heat exchangers online."

Pade lowered the volume. "I need your help. Listen to me."

"I still can't hear you—stand by."

Pade peeked out the window again. Odom was still inching forward, holding the control box in her hands as though she were offering a gift.

Gater's voice returned. "I stepped away from the exchanger impellers. What's going on?"

"I need you to override the lock on airlock Charlie-Papa Two."

"I didn't put a lock on that door."

"Odom did. Just override it."

"I thought she was napping in your quarters."

"I don't have the time to explain. I need Charlie-Papa Two open, like five minutes ago!"

"Wait! Katie hacked my ship?"

Pade bit his tongue. He heard some clicking.

"I see what she did," Gater said. "I can get it open quick and dirty or do it proper. Proper will take me a few minutes, at the very least."

Pade looked out the window. Odom was just visible; she appeared to be repeatedly pushing a button on the black box. Pade was about to switch to her channel when Odom jolted and flung the box away. She raised her hands, palms out, and backed up in a crouch.

He had to get through the door. "Do it now!" Pade ordered.

"It'll be out of commission for half an—"

"Now!"

"Done."

The door unlocked, breaking the seal. Air rushed by Pade and through the gaps around the door.

"You'll have to push it the rest of the way," Gater said. "What's going on? Do you need me to come up there?"

"No! No. Get the power back on. I got this."

"Alright. With any luck it shouldn't be much longer."

Pade planted his feet. Using the magnetic boots for leverage, he reached into the gap with his fingers, and pulled on the door. He worked his body through the opening as soon as there was enough room.

Odom was running in a crouch toward the back of the shipping container, doing as well as anyone could while wearing mag-boots. The dragon flew by her, crashing into the side of the container, its claws and tail scrambling and waving around, looking for purchase. Its movements were sluggish, its reactions slow for a droid, and Pade wondered if the cold was indeed hampering it.

He unslung Happy and pulled her to his shoulder, trying to get the red dot on the dragon. But it thrashed around, and there was little to target from his position on the catwalk. Besides, Odom was still in the area. He couldn't afford a miss or a ricochet hitting her. He pulled the weapon down and clanked along the catwalk to get closer, switching his comms to communicate with Odom.

"I'm coming, doc."

Odom screamed as she ran, again disappearing at the far end of the container. The fear in her voice, the terror in her breathing, echoed loud and clear through Pade's comms device.

The dragon, now alone, had managed to right itself on the side of the lab. Pade took aim and fired as the dragon launched toward the back and Odom. The NED round sparked harmlessly as it struck the floor, and dozens of blue electrical arcs fingered out over an area about a meter wide.

Pade readied a second shot, placing the red dot on the dragon, but the droid had already launched behind the container before he could shoot. Neither Odom nor the dragon was visible.

Odom's screams nearly froze his heart.

"Hold on!" Pade shouted. "I'm almost there." He stepped onto the catwalk's railing, aimed his body, and launched toward the back of the container, tucking as he flew across the bay in the zero gravity. Odom screamed and grunted and shouted on the comm channel. It was clear she was struggling with something.

"No. Stop," she pleaded. Her voice became frail and light.

Pade landed feet first and twisted, aiming his shotgun, looking for his target.

Odom, facing Pade, stood on the back of the container as though it were the ground, her body parallel to the cargo bay's floor. Each boot's sole spanned a small, dark gap between the container's door and the door frame. She held her left arm against the side of her suit, where a red stain grew. Her right hand was pressed there too.

"Help me," she said.

The dragon's claws, caught in the gap between the door and frame, raked and pushed and gouged the metal. They blocked the door from closing. Two red eyes inside the container pierced the darkness of the slit and locked on Pade.

"The boots are on EV lock," Odom said, "but I don't know..." She stopped, seeming to lack the breath. Her eyes were half closed.

Extra-Vehicular lock was used to keep someone from floating off the ship while they worked in zero or near-zero gravity environments. It was not intended to keep a malfunctioning murder-droid locked inside a container. Pade lunged for the door and placed the tip of Happy's barrel through the gap where he'd last seen the red eyes. He fired repeatedly into the lab, feeling the recoil but hearing almost no sound.

The claws slipped away.

Pade pulled his weapon free, and the door slammed shut. He threw the latch, locking the dragon inside, in case it was still alive.

"I don't want to die," Odom rasped.

Pade knelt and caught sight of blood spraying like paint from the side of her suit. The red mist froze into sand-like grains, bounced off the floor, and floated away. There was no way to tell how much blood she had lost this way. He searched her sides, moving around her hands and arms as needed, and located several tears in the suit. Blood gathered along those edges in some areas and sprayed from others. He grabbed Odom's suit emergency kit and pulled out the patches designed to cover and seal small punctures and cuts.

There would not be enough.

She must have seen it in his eyes. "I don't want to die," she repeated.

"You're going to be alright," Pade said, pulling the patches from his own kit. "You're going to be alright."

The patches, intended for minor accidents sustained while working outside the ship, were only for small tears and holes, not the large gaps the dragon had ripped into Odom's suit. Pade would have to make do with what he had. He peeled the patches from their backing, doing his best to stop the loss of atmosphere. Odom winced as he placed each one.

He gently moved her arm up so he could work the suit's controls and pulled up the life support readings. The suit's power level was nominal, and the patches allowed the interior to reach a functioning atmosphere. But oxygen continued to seep out, and the spare tank could barely maintain the limited atmosphere Odom needed. It would not last long.

"You're gonna be alright," he said again.

"Stop lying. I'm not stupid."

"I know. Several advanced degrees."

"No." She smiled weakly. "I have a HUD in here, dumbass."

Pade chuckled. Odom, pale and tired-looking, seemed to be breathing easier, and humor was good at times like this. He thought for a moment, remembering the airlock, but he recalled Gater's words—it was out of commission.

He smiled. There was something else about the airlock that could help.

"You may have degrees," Pade said, "but I have several more suits with patches in the airlock. We'll get you patched up. Don't worry."

Pade flipped her controls until the suit's systems were accessible. She didn't resist. He de-magnetized the boots, and Odom floated off the container, hovering over the floor. Grabbing the handle on the back of her suit, he started for the ladder to the catwalk, pulling her behind him like a balloon.

They had just arrived at the base of the ladder when Odom's voice squeaked across his comms.

"Captain."

But Pade was more concerned by the tremors in the ladder's steel handrails. They vibrated in pulses, like someone was striking a hammer somewhere on the catwalk.

"Captain." Her voice, stronger and more urgent, tugged at him.

Pade turned, his eyes following Odom's pointed finger to the shipping container. Its once uniform side displayed several bulges, and the seam along one edge had broken apart, exposing a nine- or ten-centimeter gap.

Through that gap stared red eyes.

"We gotta jettison that thing," Pade snapped.

"I can do that," Odom said. She winced as she spoke.

"But...?"

"I'm running out of air. You get the patches. I'll run the cargo system. I know how." Though weak, her voice was determined.

Pade stared at her. Something about the plan made him worry. After all, she didn't want the dragon to be hurt. Her eyelids were heavy, and she seemed paler than before. He was concerned about her blood loss.

"I promise, Captain. I'll come back and collect it later."

Another vibration in the railing reminded Pade they didn't have time to argue.

"Do it." He charged up the ladder to the catwalk as she hobbled to the loading controls at the back of the cargo bay.

Before heading into the open airlock, he looked back over his shoulder. Odom was hidden by the catwalk, but the bay's main door had opened, and the loading platform was extending toward the blackness that lay beyond. A blackness dotted by innumerable points of light, like the eyes of souls that had gone before and now watched and waited.

A chill ran up his neck. He paused.

"Doing great so far," he said, hoping to hear her voice.

"I... remember," she said wearily.

He hustled into the airlock and punched the codes for the lockers, grabbing repair kit after repair kit until he was sure he had enough. He slung the medical bag over his shoulder and returned to the cargo bay.

Pade stepped back onto the catwalk in time to see the container rolling along the conveyor system toward the open bay door. The dragon had opened the seam wide enough to force an entire arm out. The top of its head was wedged in the opening. Its jagged metal teeth bit and tugged on the edges of the container that kept it trapped.

By the time Pade reached the bottom of the ladder, the container had run off the platform and was floating away into the emptiness. The dragon's metal arm glinted in the light shed by the cargo bay.

"Great job," Pade said. "We can shut the door now."

Odom stood by the control panel, her hand hovering, unable to find the right button.

"This one," Pade said as he punched the control to retract the platform and shut the door. "Now, let's get that suit patched up."

Odom stood there, unmoving. Her eyes staring, unfocused.

"Doc. Doc. Talk to me." Pade shook her, but she did not react. "Doc. Don't do this."

He pulled her arm up to look at the controls. It showed she should have enough air to breathe, just barely. But her vital signs had terminated. A check of the history showed a loss of blood and a drop in blood pressure before cardiac arrest.

He grabbed her helmet and placed his face shield against hers, listening, hoping for some sound that would prove her suit computer wrong.

Nothing.

Pade let her go. "Oh, doc."

The comms beeped. Gater was trying to reach him. Pade fumbled with his controls and switched channels.

"Go ahead," he said.

It was quiet in the background. "Power is up. Let me know when it's safe to send the patch bots to the damaged conduit."

"Send 'em."

"Done. Starting life support too. Hey, is Katie with you?"

Pade turned away from Odom. The container was still visible beyond the slowly closing door. He took a breath, trying to think of how to tell Gater. He couldn't. Not yet.

"Yeah."

"Don't give her too much grief for locking that door. I really like her."

The stars seemed dimmer outside. He felt alone.

"I know."

IV

Dragon's Clutch

Valerie Brown

Chapter the First: My Decision

Burning embers were all that remained of the best dragon in the world.

I stood at the front of the funeral pyre, where Umbra's head used to be. Dragons don't leave bones behind. They're born of fire and magic, and return to such when properly memorialized.

The noon sun blazed overhead, drying the tears on my cheeks. Black smoke from the pyre mixed with that of the wildfires nearby. It was a beautiful, hot day.

"Alizeh!" My father called from the rear of the pyre. "Come see!"

Mother and I ran to him.

Father pointed into the middle, where Umbra's body had been. Peeking from beneath a mound of gray ashes were four brown eggs.

We gasped.

Mother turned to a servant. "Bring an iron chest. Make haste!"

I knelt on the simmering coals and inspected the clutch of eggs. They were slightly longer and more ovular than chicken eggs, speckled, and shined like the polished flint and magnesium beaded bracelets dangling from my wrists.

"Are they hot?" Mother stooped over my shoulder.

"Scalding. Luckily." I sat back on my heels. The knees of my pants were singed.

"Stoke the embers, Alizeh." Father stroked the shell of one of the eggs with gentle fingers.

I carefully wedged my hand into the coals beneath the eggs. The contact allowed me control over the spirit of the flame and I willed the heat to grow. A small bed of flames ignited.

A group of servants finally returned, carrying a heavy iron chest. They set the chest on hot ashes first, allowing it to heat up, then Father and I filled the bottom with blinking red coals. We nestled the eggs carefully inside before taking them home.

The House of Char and Milkstone was built from enormous bricks of polished white milkstone, though you'd never know it by just a glance. Wildfires raged constantly in these parts, dusting the world in soot, leaving our home blackened. Occasionally a heavy rain washed it clean, but rain was rare here.

"Alizeh." My father beckoned me to him as he tromped through a patch of dry waving grasses, Mother at his side. "The dragon's clutch must be taken to the volcanic islands in the Obsidian Sea if they are to hatch. The perytons can't fly such a journey on their own." He stopped walking, his gaze softened. "The time has come for you to choose a husband. You've received offers. I will hear your decision at supper."

I spent the ensuing hours poring over the offers of marriage I had received since coming of age. There were four. One from each of the other Endowments: Water Wielders, Creature Commanders, Wind Whisperers, and Mineral Masters. Spark Swayers—like my family—were usually in high demand; the ability to wield fire was useful on land or sea and at any time of year.

But which Endowment would help me cross the seas and reach the volcanic islands? Mineral Masters and Wind Whisperers dominated the west, in the opposite direction I needed to go. I sighed as I set both of those offers aside.

That left Water Wielders and Creature Commanders. Now I was making progress. The offer from the Water Wielders was to marry a fifteen-year-old boy, son of the admiral of a mighty fleet. I cringed just a little. This particular fleet wasn't of the most reputable nature, and marrying a boy wasn't exactly what I'd been hoping for.

Now time to look over the Creature Commanders' offer. I had never given much thought to marrying into this family. I loved animals—dragons and perytons mostly—but the gift of animal persuasiveness had never drawn me in, not like the power to move the wind or to command an entire sea. Still, this offer was good. The lord was grown, he owned his own ships, and his home was on the coast. Check. Check. Check.

I hemmed and hawed for only a moment. It was clear that a marriage into a *good* family on the coast—even an animal-loving one—was ideal compared to marrying into a fleet of pirates. Besides, living on the sea would dampen the opportunities I had to use my powers—for no matter how useful the gift of fire was, using my talents on wooden ships could ultimately yield problems.

I had selected my man.

At dinner, my parents and I sat around the ancient oblong table carved from imported volcanic rock. I waited anxiously for Father to ask me who I wanted to marry. Once the first course was served, he finally looked my way.

"Well, Alizeh, who have you chosen?"

My throat went dry. In that moment, I was sealing my fate to a man I didn't know. I gulped some wine, but finally, I found my voice. "I've chosen to accept the offer from Lord Eloy MacMurray of the House of Pearl and Bone. His home is on the coast, only a short distance from the Obsidian Sea and the volcanic islands."

Father leaned back in his seat, a pensive expression on his face. He was the quintessential Firelander with an olive complexion and hair and eyes the color of soot. I looked like Mother, a Wind Whisperer from the west, with honey-blonde hair and pale gray eyes. With my mother's looks and my father's Endowment, I was the best of both my parents.

Finally, Father said, "Lord MacMurray is a landowner, not a seaman."

I swallowed a mouthful of herbed potatoes. "He has his own ships; with the majority of his estate along the coast, his personal flotilla is fairly substantial."

Mother wiped her lips with a pale linen napkin. "Lord Mac-Murray's house is not on good terms with the Fleet of Misty Swells, which resides offshore of the Pearl and Bone estate. You will have to cross them to reach the volcanic islands."

I sipped my spiced wine for courage. "No one is on good terms with Misty Swells. They're pirates!"

Mother nodded, a slight grin on her lips. Father brushed crumbs off his fingers. They gazed at each other, silently conversing in the way parents do right in front of their children. Mother reached out and took his hand. The two smiled.

Father picked up his knife. "We accept your decision." His eyes twinkled. "But a Creature Commander?" He chuckled as he cut a slice of charred pheasant. "You'll be sleeping with rodents and mopping up droppings half your life."

Mother swatted him playfully with her napkin. "Don't say that."

I rolled my eyes, but a twinge of disgust ignited in my stomach. "I'm sure Lord MacMurray has *people* for that."

Chapter the Second: An Unwelcome Missive

Not a month later, I watched a party fly in on the backs of my father's perytons. The group consisted of my father, Lord Mac-Murray, and his lordship's numerous wedding attendants.

I bit my lip. I would be leaving my home in two days' time. Nerves simmered in my stomach, leaving me nauseous. The wedding plans had been settled so quickly, I'd hardly had time to prepare myself for the changes to come.

My father's herd of perytons touched down in the main courtyard. I had the perfect view from my bedroom window. The winged elks pawed the earth, shook out their sapphire wings, and gently nudged the dismounting wedding guests with long, gilded antlers.

And there was Lord MacMurray amid it all, talking with my father. His bald pate mimicked the shine of the Great Milkstone in the sky. Strange tattoos peeped from the neckline of his riding clothes.

My heartbeat flickered. Lord MacMurray was...unexpectedly handsome. I had thought, given his rugged coastal existence, that he would be of a weathered nature, but he seemed only lacking in the rich color I associated with my days in the sun. I smoothed my blouse and checked the folds of my skirt. There were only minimal soot stains along the bottom hem; this was a special occasion.

An elegantly dressed woman of a mature disposition approached Lord MacMurray, and based on the curve of her smile and the loving gaze she imparted on the young lord, I suspected her to be his mother. She too showcased a series of dark tattoos along her thin arms and fingers.

The nervous simmering in my stomach was now a dull sizzle. Perhaps the smiles of these visitors were genuine and I needn't be shy. Taking a deep breath, I left my suite and descended into the great hall to await their entrance alongside my mother. She held my hand in silence, but smiled at me often.

The sconces in the main parlor had been lit with precious dragon's flame—the remnants of our beloved Umbra—casting a greenish hue along the walls. The dark flames hardly illuminated the space, but the hearth burned bright enough to compensate somewhat for the overall dimness.

When the whole assembly entered, Father made Mother's introduction first, then gestured to me.

"Lord Eloy MacMurray and his honored mother, Lady Keavy MacMurray, let me introduce to you my daughter, Lady Alizeh Edan of the House of Char and Milkstone."

Lord MacMurray and I were wed the next day in a field beneath the Great Ember. Wildfires raged on the horizon, raising a black curtain into the pale blue sky.

My gown was sewn of soft green linen and tied about the waist with a dark green embroidered sash. The hem of my dress was stained black by the ashes on the ground, as were my satin-strapped sandals. In the tradition of all Firelanders, I had shadowed my eyelids with fine powdered ash to honor the temper of the land.

Before the ceremony started, Father slipped newly made bracelets of magnesium and flint onto my wrists before kissing my cheek. Mother wove a dozen pink flowers into my wavy hair. During the ceremony, she kept the breezes cool and directed the smoke away from our guests.

Lord MacMurray and I clasped hands while standing on an ancient slab of imported pale milkstone. Generations of my family had been married on this site, honoring the gods of day and night.

Assorted yellow birds sat on Lord MacMurray's broad shoulders. He was debonair in a loose-fitting white shirt with a strange craggy rock fastened at the collar. His dark pants were practical, but new. Black tattoos slid from beneath his collar and trailed down his strong forearms. I chewed on my lip as the priest mused on commitment and loyalty and reverence to the Great Ember. My cheeks burned when he brought up being fruitful. Lord MacMurray's complexion darkened a shade as well.

The culmination of our ceremony involved a sharing of Endowments. I had preselected and cut the driest of imported hardwoods and laid them out in a circle. Kneeling beside the wood, I banged my beaded wrists together, creating a shower of sparks, then stuck my fingers in the winking tinder. Flames licked up. I made them dance like two people—like I hoped to dance with Lord MacMurray before the night was out. Then I turned the flames into birds, like the ones on his shoulders. The birds sizzled as they took flight, leaving the fire, sprinkling the air with specks of orange before burning out.

When it was his turn, Lord MacMurray brushed the small birds off his shoulders, then beckoned them back with open palms. The birds flopped onto their backs, where he proceeded to juggle them. I giggled. The powers of a Creature Commander were rather charming.

Lord MacMurray tossed a small sparrow to me. I caught it. The wedding attendants chuckled as the bird shook out its feathers, got to its feet, and flew back to my new husband.

The ceremony was followed by an enormous banquet held right there in the field beneath the Great Milkstone. Tall waxen tapers cast subtle light over an array of foods. Steam rose from thick cuts of pork and fowl. Boiled carrots dappled with green herbs shared platters with smashed potatoes topped with floral butter. Fragrant tea and spiced red wine were poured for everyone. Lord MacMurray sat next to me.

The rest of the night was wonderful: dancing, dessert, lively conversation... But let me just say, kissing Lord MacMurray in the moonlight was the delight of the evening.

We were awoken the next morning to rapid knocking at the door. Groggy as we were from the spiced wine, it took us a moment to realize we were being summoned.

I strolled lazily to the door. My lady's maid handed me a small rolled scroll. "For *Lord* MacMurray," she whispered, "this just arrived." Bowing, she turned away.

I handed the missive to my husband, who was rubbing his eyes as he sat up. He stilled as he read, clenching his jaw.

"What is it?"

He huffed as he threw the paper down. "We must depart. The Fleet of Misty Swells has taken advantage of my absence and attacked my home." Eloy rose. I blushed at his nudity, but he didn't seem to notice. He grabbed his pants and slid them on. "Our kraken, Pearl, is missing from her keep. She is due to give birth soon— I must return home at once to rescue her."

"My things are almost entirely packed as it is." I reached over and yanked the long ribbon by the door, ringing for service. "Instead of leaving after supper, we can go before lunch."

We departed for the coast with the gift of a small herd of perytons from my parents. We took turns between riding the perytons and the horses, keeping everyone as fresh as possible with as little rest as necessary. We also traded bovines at each village to haul my heated iron carriage that housed the dragon's eggs.

Two weeks of harried travel brought us to a great stony land by the sea. All the warm colors of my homeland were replaced by cool grays and greens, subtle purples and blues. My new home, the House of Pearl and Bone, stood on the edge of a jagged cliff. A cold wind gusted off the sea, accompanied by mist, fog, and the smell of salt. The house itself was made of granite and partially carved into the cliffs. Everything was considerably wet.

At the main door, we were greeted by a row of anxious servants who eagerly ushered us inside. It was nearly nightfall and we were all starving, but Eloy needed to inspect the keep himself.

He pulled down a torch from the main entryway and our whole party cut through many fine rooms and stony hallways before finally exiting through an exterior passage, where the sea winds whipped with aching cold. A narrow stairwell descended into the cliffs, offering a brief reprieve, but smelled of stagnant water.

Eloy held my hand as we descended, keeping me steady down the slick stairs. Everyone else was quick and agile; accustomed to such conditions.

At the bottom, we stepped out of the tunnel and into the wind and salty spray. Eloy's torch threatened to go out. I clutched his hand for balance, and to steady my nerves. The ground was wet, the wind wild, and there was an altogether otherness about the gray place.

A doorway loomed ahead in a massive stone cliff. We entered the aquatic keep: a cavernous space with a deep black pool leading out into the Briny Bite. Eloy lowered the torch into a pit against the wall. Soft yellow flames illuminated his face. His wild gaze took in the status of the keep.

Charred wood floated on the surface of the water and the ceiling of the keep was covered in soot from a roaring fire. A second fire pit, located on the far side of the keep, was turned over, its coals spilled on the floor.

"Has there been a sighting of Pearl since the attack?" Eloy asked an attendant as he pulled off his shirt, revealing the dark oceanic tattoos I had explored shyly on our wedding night.

The man shook his head as he draped my husband's garment over his arm. "No, milord."

Eloy dove into the freezing water. His mother, Lady Keavy, took my hand. Her tattooed fingers were cold, but firm. "If Pearl is nearby, she will come to him."

Our group peered anxiously into the black depths. Waves churned angrily, and for a moment I worried. "Eloy is a strong swimmer, yes?"

His mother squeezed my fingers. "He can hold his breath for five minutes. Do not worry."

I nodded, only slightly assuaged.

My husband's pale bald head popped out of the water a moment later. There was a large many-legged beast wrapped around him.

"Is this Pearl?" I had thought krakens to be much bigger.

"No, this is an octopus. Pearl isn't here." Eloy gently untangled the squirmy tentacles from his body and climbed out of the water. He walked to the fire and held his arms over the flames. One of his men threw a dry blanket over his shoulders. The rest of his household moved in unison, concealing him from the winds with an additional woven blanket and providing him with dry clothes. When he emerged, he shivered, then hastily fastened a heavy green tunic around his shoulders.

"My lord," I said as I took his side, "I am accustomed to the idea that a dragon may come and go as it pleases. While one may reside with us for a time, there is always a chance it won't come back, especially once it leaves to mate. Is it possible that Pearl has only left due to fright?"

Eloy shook his head. "Pearl and her line have always been here; since the beginning of recorded time. She does leave occasionally, but her absences coincide with hunting, like the yearly ridged whale migration. Our records show that krakens only mate once in a lifetime. And she has already returned from that venture." He balled his fists. "The Fleet of Misty Swells has gone too far. Their leviathans drive away the tuna. Their men steal from the fishermen, and frighten the villagers. I have tried to negotiate with Admiral Bacchas, but no more."

Eloy summoned one of his tattooed men, a tall sailor with a muscled build.

"Ready the ships."

"Aye, milord."

Grabbing my hand, Eloy led our whole group back into the biting cold, practically dragging me up the wet stairs toward the house. "I must set out for Milkstone Isle to see if I can persuade the hydra to join me."

Eloy's mother scrambled up the stairs behind us, nudging men out of her way. Her voice echoed along the passage. "The hydra is unpredictable, my son. Surely you can find a group of griffons or a unicorn to assist you."

My husband chuckled. We entered the main dining room and he handed off the torch to one of his men. Running a hand over his bald head, he sighed cajolingly. "Oh, Mother, if only it were that easy." His humor subsided. "The hydra is strong enough to fight off the leviathans and keep them from sinking my ships. I must have it on my team if we are to engage the Fleet in battle out in the open sea."

Lady Keavy nodded, though her complexion paled considerably.

Eloy led me to our bedchamber and adjoining suite. He hurriedly packed a trunk with spare clothes.

"I'm coming with you." My trunks had already been delivered to our room, so I searched until I found a pair of linen pants and a matching blue blouse. "Hydras are loch-based dragons. I know dragons."

His eyes met mine and he smirked. "Yes, you must come, I think, but... The hydra is about as friendly as a—"

"Dragon?" I smiled. "Believe me, I can help. Is this hydra male or female?"

"Male."

I combed my hair and pinned it back out of my eyes. "Do you still have the bulls that pulled the iron carriage?"

He nodded.

"Bring one with us, but do nothing until I say so."

"Yes, milady." He grinned as he offered me a quilted vest matching his own. "Your new wardrobe will be ready soon."

"That will be a relief." I slid into the vest, savoring its warmth. "We need to bring my dragon's eggs with us, too."

"That may be unwise. If we should fail in our strike against the Fleet, the eggs will be lost to sea—or worse, to the admiral."

I huffed, but decided to press the issue. "One of the eggs is dead, and another will be soon." I shook my head. "It is a risk worth taking to hopefully not lose them all."

Chapter the Third: Loch

We set sail before dawn. Murky waves crashed against the hull as we set off for Milkstone Isle. I studied a weathered map spread across Eloy's navigation table. The isle was small, only a mile off-shore, due east. We arrived just as the Great Ember crested above the waves.

Lord MacMurray directed his men to the western side of the island, where a deep loch allowed the ship to approach the shore and drop anchor. Despite the sunrise, there was still a morning gloom over the place. A heavy mist surrounded the island, but I could just make out the mouth of an enormous cave off the rocky white beach.

"Are those all milkstones?" I strained my eyes to see through the mist.

Eloy put an arm around my shoulder. "They are."

"I should like to collect a few before we depart."

He rubbed his jaw. "Perhaps after we enlist the hydra?"

"Agreed." I leaned into his embrace.

Our men pushed a heavy wooden plank over the edge of the deck. The huge platform tilted toward the beach, where it embedded in the loose stones. Eloy went below-decks to get the bull—

whose mournful bellows echoed even now—and escorted him down the ramp.

The bull's brown eyes glazed over when it was near my husband, and he followed him like a lovesick puppy. Guilt charred my heartstrings, but... sacrifices had to be made, to save not only my dragon eggs, but Eloy's kraken.

I lit a torch from the storeroom before descending the platform. The milkstones clunked beneath my feet like the smooth river stones I'd seen out west. Our group made a lot of noise. We didn't have the element of surprise.

About thirty feet from the mouth of the cave I gestured for our men to halt. My husband and I continued, bull in tow.

The cave was dark, quiet. In fact, the whole island was eerily silent. A stiff breeze brought the smell of decay and dank water from the home of the hydra.

I stepped in front of my husband and gripped the lit end of my torch. The flames crawled onto my hand. I threw the torch into the darkness ahead.

It clattered on the rocky floor between the clawed, webbed feet of the giant dragon.

The hydra had six heads, and six pairs of eyes, all glaring at us. We had certainly awoken it with our presence. Dragons didn't like their naps disturbed.

One of the center heads opened its toothy mouth. An ominous green flame tickled at the back of its throat. Before it could fire, I raised my hands and shot two columns of flame directly into the sky.

The hydra closed its many maws and watched. I threw balls of fire into the air, higher and higher, until the hydra craned its many necks to see them sizzle out in the sky. Edging its hulking body out into the open, the creature was a daunting spectacle. Deep purple scales ran the length of its body, while its stomach was almost pure white. Fins cut back from the neck and ran all the way down to its muscled tail, which flattened toward the tip. The hydra's irises were narrowed at the ends, like Umbra's, but the eye shape was more bulbous and surrounded with dark scales, like the eye ash I'd worn on my wedding day.

Once I knew I had the hydra's full attention, I called over my shoulder to Eloy, "Leave the bull!"

There wasn't time to indulge in guilt. Besides, I'd done the same for Umbra at her hatch-day celebration. Dragons liked a good show—and a juicy snack.

Eloy tossed the rope and ran back to his men. The bull stared longingly after him, but before it could move, I turned and blasted the bovine with the fullest heat I could produce. I didn't want the animal to suffer, plus, the bigger the blaze, the happier the dragon.

Eloy and his men threw up their arms against the heat and stumbled back several more feet. The bull bucked and screamed before collapsing.

I lowered my arms, breathing heavily. All was quiet except for the crackle of fire. The smell of cooked meat filled the air. I centered myself in front of the bull. The hydra's twelve eyes followed me. Opening my arms, I bowed low, then backed away, giving the dragon full view of its breakfast.

When I reached Eloy's side I exhaled with relief. The hydra tromped forward, hauling its massive snake-like body behind its two front legs. "You can approach him now." I wiped the sweat from my brow, smearing dark soot across my skin. "He'll be more open to your connection while he's eating."

Eloy's eyes were wide, his mouth slightly agape. "That was amazing." He kissed my cheek before moving alongside the dragon.

The hydra had heads to spare. Two watched my husband approach while the rest feasted on the roasted carcass. Eloy walked with confidence, held himself strongly. He placed his hands on the hydra's side. One of the heads twitched, cutting its gaze across to see Eloy more clearly.

Eloy closed his eyes and breathed deep. Despite all my experience, closing my eyes in the presence of an unknown dragon was not something *I'd* do. But the hydra sighed, leaned into his touch, and returned its attention to eating.

After a few moments, Eloy grabbed the long strip of fin running the length of the hydra's body and pulled himself onto the muscled back. I cringed. That was a level of comfort not usually achieved so quickly with a dragon. Yes, I could sit upon Umbra, but we had been raised together. This was different. For the first time, I was truly in awe of the Creature Commander Endowment.

"The hydra will help us," called Eloy from his mount. "We have shared thoughts. He wants to kill Misty Swells' leviathans, who frequently invade his hunting territory. We must aid him in this endeavor."

I exchanged a tentative look with a few men. The plan had been to engage the hydra to take on the leviathans while we battled the humans of Misty Swells. Now we had to save a kraken, kill leviathans, *and* get my eggs to the volcanic islands without being killed. It seemed to me our luck was strained.

I tried not to let my nerves get the better of me. "Did the hydra give you its name?"

Eloy smirked. "Our connection doesn't work that way, but I'm sure he won't mind you calling him something. What shall it be?"

The hydra ripped a huge chunk of meat off the bull's remains. Cooked brown blood pooled beneath the feast and covered his many mouths. He certainly wasn't cute. The dragon was strong and dark, like the sea.

"What about Loch?"

"That's perfect." Eloy patted the hydra affectionately along one of its many necks. The dragon barely spared him a glance before focusing again on its meal. Bloodstained bones and sagging bits of flesh were all that remained of the powerful bull. The long-horned skull lay beside the body, completely detached. Eloy slid off Loch and walked to me. "He'll be finished in a moment. We should return to the ship."

Eloy's men eagerly followed orders, but I lingered to collect a few rounded samples of milkstone before boarding.

When Loch was finished, he slid into the sea like a snake. His long tail swished powerfully, gliding him through the water with speed and grace. His coloring blended with the choppy sea perfectly and I soon lost sight of him.

As we sailed deeper into the Briny Bite, I spent some time below-decks with my dragon eggs. One was dead—dull and cool to the touch. A second followed not far behind, but the other two stood a chance. If we could reach the volcanic islands within a few days, they would live.

Spreading out my moonstones in a circular formation, I set a tin plate in the middle and lit a small fire using my bracelet beads. I prayed to the Great Ember, then to the Great Milkstone. I prayed for a safe journey, for success in our ventures. My fingers blackened from drawing in the ashes.

The ship rocked gently, like a lullaby. The winds were cool and fast, taking us quickly to our destination in the middle of the Briny

Bite. When Eloy next came to me, our ships were approaching the Fleet. He knelt at my side.

"Here." I handed him a small milkstone. "For good fortune."

He tucked it into his vest, then kissed me hard right there on the floor. Our arms tangled in a passionate embrace. My heart, which I had worked so hard to calm, beat wildly.

Eloy pulled away, his green eyes bright with worry. "You must be careful, Alizeh. We stand a good chance—especially if I can free Pearl—but it'll be dangerous. If you see the admiral or his son, don't let them reach the water. They are just average men, until they make connection with their elemental Endowment."

Chapter the Fourth: A Welcome Ally

Eloy's flotilla approached the Fleet of Misty Swells with the wind full in its sails. Though it was midday, heavy gray mist concealed our approach.

Eloy checked the spyglass. "The Fleet's sails are tied up. Their ships are anchored."

In this instance, it seemed, we had the element of surprise.

The wind whipped my hair. The Great Ember burned apart the clouds just as we came within shooting range.

"Ready the canons!" Eloy donned a green tricornered hat with a white kraken sewn to the side. Men scampered below-decks. Ominous thuds sounded below our feet. A man in the crow's nest signaled the other ships. It was all hands on deck.

A huge ship loomed before us like a city at sea. It dwarfed our entire fleet.

I slid my arm around Eloy's waist. "I've never seen a ship that big."

He pulled out the spyglass once again. "The big one is called the *Kraken's Keep*." He lowered the glass. "I guess we know where the admiral's keeping Pearl." He turned back to his first mate. "Aim the cannons at the biggest ship!"

"Aye, sir!"

Word was spread among the flotilla.

Eloy squeezed my hand. "If we can compromise the hull, Pearl should be able to escape."

I nodded and anxiously checked my bracelets. They were secure, but I felt like I needed some readymade ammunition. I ran below-decks and found a lantern. Having lit the wick, I scrambled back above to stand with Eloy.

Someone had raised the alarm within Misty Swells. People swarmed above-decks like insects. I couldn't imagine how many were bustling around below.

Eloy shoved his fist in the air. "Fire!"

His cannons let loose. Their shots sped across the water and impaled the hull of the *Kraken's Keep*.

Musket fire rained down from our enemies. I crouched below the railing with my lantern. Men's shouts echoed over the choppy sea. I peeked back over the railing—only to see the sinuous snake bodies of the leviathans writhing beneath our ships.

My heart jumped into my throat as I pointed.

"I know!" Eloy gazed into the depths, his jaw set.

A round of cannon fire issued from the *Kraken's Keep*. Eloy shoved me flat against the deck as wood exploded around us. Sections of the railing disappeared and the deck was marred with gouges.

"We'll never win fighting broadside against a ship of that size." Eloy motioned to the helmsman to turn the wheel. The sails switched sides, sweeping recklessly across the deck.

Men scampered to manage the riggings as another round of musket fire rained down. Acrid smoke burned my nose before the determined wind drove it away.

Startled screams sounded from the front of our ship. Crewmen stumbled back, tumbling over fallen ropes and scattered debris as they attempted to escape. A long leviathan tail rose out of the water and wrapped around the bowsprit, tugging it downwards. Eloy climbed the railing and jumped overboard. He was gone before I could blink.

I ran to the railing near the front of the ship and peered over. Eloy's arms and legs were wrapped tightly around the body of the sea serpent. His eyes were closed. He appeared calm despite the danger.

After a moment, the leviathan released the ship and we sloshed back into a buoyant position. I threw a rope down as Eloy released the body of the creature. He grabbed on and climbed back up, sopping wet, but victorious. His lovely hat was gone.

"That was incredible!" I threw my arms around his neck. "But don't do that again."

Eloy smirked. His flotilla angled to the side of Misty Swells' standard-sized ships. The enemy's anchors were pulled, their sails released. We opened fire—but so did they. Both fleets were caught in a dangerous dance above a turmoil of sea monsters.

Loch crested the waves, the long body of a leviathan clamped in its six mouths. Blood stained the water red.

"We have to get back into position and open fire on the *Kraken's Keep*!" Eloy cupped his hands over his mouth as he yelled at the helmsman. "Keep going! Take us around to the big ship! Make haste!"

"Aye, sir!"

I peered over the railing. Loch's long body was entangled with a leviathan's. The two twisted, churning up the water. The leviathan's jaws were embedded deep into Loch's back, where he couldn't reach with his heads.

I stuffed my hand into the lantern and caught fire. "Loch!" Winding back, I threw a hot sphere of flame at the sea monsters, hitting both—but one of Loch's heads turned my way, and I knew he understood.

He overpowered the leviathan's roll, arching out of the water, leaving the sea serpent exposed. I released a column of flame, knowing dragons were immune to my Endowment. The leviathan's wet whiskers and scales finally burned. He released Loch's back.

Loch made quick work of the beast after that.

Eloy steadied me as our ship rocked in the rough waves, before yanking me along after him. Crosswinds tossed my tangled hair and I shoved it back to see where we were going. Our ship was approaching the *Kraken's Keep*, positioning to fire. "We must get the first shot," he hollered over the wind and gunfire.

"How many leviathans are there?" I gasped as I took a face full of salty spray.

"Six, I think."

"We're down two, at least."

Green flame burst out of the sea, igniting the scaled tail of a leviathan wrapped around the bowsprit of another of Eloy's ships. The sea monster screeched before diving underwater, leaving Eloy's ship afloat.

Loch dove underwater, too. His tail slapped the surface alongside the leviathan's. The two beasts disappeared into the murky depths.

The *Kraken's Keep* loomed ahead like a wooden fortress. I stepped back. "We're too close!"

"We must be close to compromise the hull at the water level." Eloy pointed. "That's where Pearl is—she must have access to seawater. Once a big enough hole has been made, she'll escape."

I realized that our proximity offered other opportunities, too. I dried my hands on my vest, retrieved the lantern, and ignited my fingers. As we pulled alongside the huge ship, we could see into the gunports. Men worked there, loading their cannons. I saw the whites of their eyes when they realized just how close we were.

I thrust out my hand and sent a crush of flame crackling against the wooden hull.

"Fire the cannons!" Eloy braced against the railing as the guns let loose.

Splinters ricocheted back at us. I squeezed my eyes shut, but never stopped shooting flame. Several cannonballs breached the *Keep*'s hull. Water started pouring in.

"Is it enough?" I double-handed the flame and finally singed some ropes higher up. Smoke breathed off the hull underneath the rigging.

"I hope so!"

Eloy grabbed me and twirled away from the *Kraken's Keep* just as it fired the full force of its cannons against us. The shots tore through our hull. The mast fell. We dodged the huge wooden pillar and landed beneath the sail. The fabric stung as it slapped against our backs, but otherwise we were fine. Eloy dragged me out from underneath.

"We're stuck now." He was breathing heavily. We were far too close to the *Kraken's Keep* and vulnerable to another attack. "We should abandon ship."

We gazed about us, but none of Eloy's ships were close. Battle raged throughout the two fleets. The seawater gurgled with fighting beasts. One of Misty Swells' ships was alight with green flame.

We turned back as the *Kraken's Keep* let out an ominous moan. "What's that noise?" I shivered, but Eloy grinned.

The *Keep*'s wood siding cracked. A long white tentacle pushed out of the lower hull, just at the waterline.

"She's coming! Pearl is breaking free!" Eloy ran to the ramp leading below-decks. "Everyone abandon ship!" He sprinted back to me, cheeks flushed, eyes shining. "When the *Keep* sinks, the undertow will take us with it. We have to go! Damn the risks."

The kraken's huge clawed arms scraped along the hull, leaving deep gouges before finally embedding in the wood. Pearl pushed another arm through the hole, breaking away more of the siding and leaving the *Kraken's Keep* with a gaping wound. The muscled arms kept coming until the hole sank beneath the water.

Men hustled around the deck while others lowered the lifeboats. Eloy pulled me toward one of the dinghies, but I dug in my heels. "I can't! My eggs!"

Together, we looked back at the *Keep*. The city-sized ship was definitely sinking. Pearl clung to the hull with five of her massive arms. The ropes I had singed had caught flame and the fire was spreading to the upper decks. Her crew was jumping overboard.

Our ship lurched backward, away from the *Kraken's Keep*. "How are we moving?" I braced against a portion of railing. The main mast was laid out our feet. We trod over it in search of the mystery. At the back of the ship we peered over the railing, into the murky gray waves. I pointed to the person in the water.

Eloy squinted, craning his body out as far as he could to see. He shook his head as he leaned back in. "Must be a Water Wielder, but he looks too young to be the admiral. Must be his son."

The boy, who I remembered was just fifteen, swam one-handed along the surface, one arm outstretched in command of his Endowment as he pushed our ship away from the *Kraken's Keep*. He was brown-skinned, black-haired, and wore what looked like a blue jacket.

A leviathan crested the water just behind him, jaws open. I snatched the lantern from the deck, took the flame, and shot a column at the sea monster. The leviathan dodged back underwater. The boy gasped, but otherwise continued his mission.

Once our ship was safely out of reach of the *Keep*'s undertow, we dropped a dinghy into the water. It dipped and rocked on the angry waves, but the admiral's son was able to climb in.

When he was safely onboard, Eloy and I eagerly shook his hand. "Thank you," I huffed with relief. "It's Guerdy Bacchas, First Son of Misty Swells, am I right?"

"You are!" The boy laughed. "A bit of a thing that was! Really got my blood pumping."

"Ours too!" Eloy grinned. "You saved our lives."

"Well, at least your ship...though it may make not it back to your estate, Lord MacMurray."

"Call me Eloy."

The boy nodded. "My father is in the *Kraken's Keep*. He will go down with the ship."

I clasped Eloy's hand, fearful of the hope swelling within me. "How do you know?"

"Because I killed him." Guerdy Bacchas shrugged. "He was a bastard." The boy flashed bright white teeth, and for an instant, he reminded me of the leviathans lurking below.

Eloy didn't seem to notice. He grabbed my waist and twirled me around.

The First Son tapped his shoulder. "As you can see, the firing from the *Keep* has ceased. Perhaps you can call off your ships? I shall do the same for the rest of the Fleet."

"Of course."

A long yellow flag was retrieved from below-decks and raised as high as we could get it without having a proper crow's nest. Guerdy Bacchas took a whistle from his interior breast pocket and blew a series of notes that echoed over the sea. Within a few moments, all firing ceased.

In the eerie silence that followed, Pearl fully escaped the belly of the *Kraken's Keep*. She gripped the hull with her clawed tentacles, tilting the massive ship off its center. Men by the dozen were diving into the cold depths of the Briny Bite.

"I do wish I could have kept her," sighed Guerdy, then he checked himself. "The ship, I mean. The *Kraken's Keep* was the first of her kind. An entire city built on the water. Truly a feat of human ingenuity—even if it was my father's ingenuity."

"She was magnificent," consoled Eloy. "Perhaps you can build another? But..." He folded his arms. "Maybe without the kraken this time."

Guerdy chortled. "I warned my father not to steal her, but he underestimated you and your Endowment; a grave mistake on his part."

Loch leaped out of the water with another leviathan dangling from his many mouths. His nostrils flared in triumph; such a happy dragon.

Guerdy frowned. "Perhaps you could call off the hydra? I'm fond of the leviathans."

"I'm afraid we made a deal with him to kill all the leviathans." Eloy rubbed his chin, an apologetic lilt to his tone.

"Yes, and we promised to help, if necessary." I gazed into the seas. Wood debris, screaming men, oil, and the occasional body floated along the surface of the water.

"I raised those leviathans." Guerdy ruffled his wet black hair. "They weren't bad, you know."

"Most monsters aren't." I thought of my clutch of dragon's eggs nestled below-decks and ventured a plea to the young man. "Admiral Bacchas" —I articulated his name, recognizing his new title—"may we cross the rest of the Briny Bite to reach the volcanic islands? I have dragon eggs in need of hatching."

Guerdy smiled. "Oh, yes?" He rubbed his chin, a glint in his brown eyes—yes, there was something distinctly predatory about this young leader. "How many eggs?"

I hesitated. "Two, maybe three."

"In exchange for safe passage, as well as compensation for my assistance, I shall require a dragon." Guerdy tapped a thin silver trident hanging from his belt. "Also, such a joy will lessen the pain of losing my beloved leviathans."

Eloy turned toward me, his expression tight. My answer could redefine our relationship with the Fleet of Misty Swells—possibly bring peace between the two great houses.

Though my heart hurt, I extended my hand. "Once the eggs are hatched, I'll deliver a dragon to you on our return home."

We shook on it. Eloy kissed my temple.

As the *Kraken's Keep* slipped below the surface of the Briny Bite, Pearl's opalescent body disappeared as well. I assumed Loch had returned to Milkstone Isle, for he too had vanished. Eloy and his fleet met up and consolidated what supplies remained on as many ships as could still float, then he sent half of them home to confirm Pearl's safe arrival.

The rest of his flotilla followed us to the volcanic islands.

Chapter the Fifth: A New Ember

We spent a week anchored off the volcanic islands. I had thought that male dragons roosted willingly, but it turned out they needed a lot of persuasion. I performed another fire-dance, another sacrifice had to be secured, and Eloy had to make the connection, but at last, the eggs were successfully hatched by a willing male dragon.

In the end, out of three eggs, we ended up with two lovely female dragons. One was orange-scaled with green veining in her wings. She had one green eye and one yellow eye, and black claws. The other baby girl had black claws too, blue-scaled with black veining in the wings, and yellow eyes. I kept the orange one.

Admiral Guerdy Bacchas was thrilled with the new addition to his fleet and arranged to meet with Eloy to learn the intricacies of animal training.

Back home—strange, how soon the House of Pearl and Bone felt like home to me—I was introduced to Pearl, and she soon gave birth to a handsome male kraken.

"Are the males always red?" I folded my legs and sat next to Eloy while he dipped his hands into the frigid seawater. The pre-dawn air was cool and misty.

"Males, yes. Female coloration varies depending on the environment, though." After a moment, the tip of a long white clawed tentacle slithered out of the water and curled around Eloy's body. "Good morning, Pearl." Eloy ran his hand down her arm, patting affectionately. Then a long, slender red tentacle slid out, just like its mother's. Eloy playfully tugged at the tentacles wrapped around his body. Pearl's baby brought two more out of the water just to hold him still.

My dragon nipped at a rogue red tentacle that curled our way. I hesitantly patted the slimy arm, which swatted my dragon right off my shoulder.

"Don't be alarmed, Coral." I held out my hand and she flew back, landing on my shoulder. She snapped her small jaws at the tentacle. I chuckled. "It seems the children are getting along."

Eloy grinned, then twisted out of Pearl's embrace. Leaving his feet dangling in the water, he leaned back and wrapped an arm around my shoulder. Coral bristled at first, but refused to be dislodged from her perch a second time.

"She and Scorch will be best mates, I think." He stroked my dragon's back, using his powers to lessen her agitation. She crooned in a most unladylike fashion before sliding into his lap.

"I guess this is what it's like living with a Creature Commander. I shall always be second best."

"Don't be jealous, milove." Eloy leaned over and kissed my cheek. "She is weak against my charms."

I rolled my eyes, but smiled. "While we're on the subject of babies… I have been nursing an ember of my own."

Eloy sat up, squinting thoughtfully. "Nursing an ember?" He shook his head. "I'm afraid I don't know your Firelander expressions."

I cleared my throat, relishing the sweet news I was about to deliver. "It is only that Coral and Scorch will have a playmate come the harvest."

Realization dawned in my husband's eyes. He sucked in a breath. "You're pregnant!"

I nodded. He kissed me, nearly squishing Coral, who coughed in alarm.

"The child will be a Spark Swayer, naturally." I tossed my hair, baiting Eloy for a response.

"Nonsense," he grinned. "The child will inherit his father's Endowment."

"*His* already? My, aren't we confident."

We chuckled together. Eloy caressed my cheek. "Let's compromise. You give me a boy and he can have any Endowment you choose."

I rubbed his hand. "I'll put in a good word with the Great Ember; although, if I pray to the Great Milkstone, I may get a girl."

The playfulness in his gaze subsided. Eloy simply looked happy as he kissed me in the golden dawn rising out of the Briny Bite.

V

Tales for Young Dragons

Ivy Hamid

From the Editor

*B*urning embers are all that remain of the history of our species. *Our stories have been retold many times, but only by lower creatures, who degrade the heroes of the past and mock their essential draconian nature. If we want young dragons to benefit from the wisdom of their ancestors, we need to reclaim our stories, correct the factual inaccuracies, and recount them in the fresh, modern style that resonates with the youth of today. Correctly presented, this foundational literature cannot help but inspire young minds. It will also provide the moral guidance so sorely needed by the young dragons of today. It is time to reignite those embers and take pride in our culture. Let us celebrate, for ourselves and our children, the essence of what makes us dragons.*

Once upon a time, not so very long ago, there lived a kind and noble dragon named Euphrene. Her home was on the coast of Libya, overlooking the beautiful Mediterranean Sea. It was a comfortable cave, facing east to catch the rising sun and tastefully decorated with potted plants and macramé wall hangings.

Every day, Euphrene emerged from her cave, stretched her wings, and took her morning glide over the sea. Passing the coast of Crete, she waved to her friends the sirens, who loafed around the beach drinking coffee and working on their tans. Then she returned to her cave for her eleven o'clock tea, and to catch up on her reading of *Eat, Prey, Love*. When it was time for lunch, she strolled out into the verdant fields and plucked a few fragrant sheep. As night fell, she settled down at the entrance to her cave. Gazing up at stars as bright as diamonds, she dreamed of one day having a hoard as magnificent as the one strewn across the heavens.

Her mother, Dorcas, had raised her very carefully. Before Dorcas ran away with a Babylonian demon, she had explained to her daughter what being a real dragon meant—being kind and respectful, and amassing a fortune in gold and non-negotiable bonds. Diamonds and rubies were also mentioned. Euphrene's mother was of the opinion that these might be worth investigating, especially if the gold market continued to fluctuate as it had ever since the capital of the Roman Empire moved over to this new place called Constantinople.

But at this moment, Euphrene, in the heady intoxication of youth, was reveling in the simple pleasures. She frolicked in fields thick with sheep, not giving a single thought to how she was going to accumulate the necessary assets against the "golden" years of her life. Had she but known what trials awaited her, she would have behaved differently. But she didn't—and thereby landed herself in the tightest spot that any dragon has ever been in, as you shall hear.

Sheep are quite plentiful in the fields of Libya, but dragons, especially young, growing dragons, have healthy appetites. I myself have known a young dragon to consume seventeen hamburgers and twenty orders of French fries in a single sitting, followed by a dozen Baked Apple Pies™. And I was not at all ill afterward.

But we were talking about the burgeoning appetite of young Euphrene. After a few hundred years, two sheep a day became five. Then five became ten. Euphrene grew into a lovely young dragon with three horns on her snout, a row of perfectly curved spines all the way down her back, and the sharpest fangs in the Northern Hemisphere.

But sheep were not as plentiful as they had been. ("Overharvesting" might best describe the situation.) And soon, Euphrene found herself running low on groceries.

Now, you may say what you like about humans, but the ones that nested inland from Euphrene's coastal home were brighter than your average specimens. They realized that such a charming and noble dragon could not be left to starve, so they began to supplement Euphrene's menu with their own offspring. Euphrene, of course, appreciated this gesture. Such high-quality protein added to the luster of her purple scales and the glint of her fine green eyes.

But one day—one fateful day—a child appeared that Euphrene simply could not eat. She was thin and bony, smelled like onions, and was a hardcore gum chewer.

"Well?" said this child, hands on hips and jaws gently grinding. "Aren'tcha gonna eat me?"

Euphrene looked at the creature in horror. "I... Well, perhaps not today."

"Why not?"

"I feel," whispered Euphrene, backing away from the stench, "that I have rather lost my appetite."

"But I'm a princess," declared the child. "Ya gotta eat me. Them's the rules."

At this moment, a knight in shining armor rode up. In his hand he held a white banner emblazoned with a red cross. The same design adorned the front of his long, flowing tunic.

171

"What's all this?" he demanded, pushing back his helmet so he could see better. "Are you eating this child, you horrible monster?"

"No," said Euphrene.

"Yes," insisted the child. "I'm a princess and that's a dragon—and it's gonna eat me, whether it wants to or not." She glared at Euphrene with her hard little eyes.

The knight noted the child's sparkly pink gown and plastic wand with a star on top. "I suppose you *might* be a princess," he conceded.

"Sure I am. I'm Princess Ringarosy. The king's my pop. He's gonna be mighty sore if this dragon don't eat me. He's gonna blow his toot!" At this the child sniggered. "Mighty funny, akshully. He sent me out here to appetize this dragon, and now the dragon don't wanna be appetized."

"Appeased," murmured Euphrene.

"Huh?"

"I think the word you want is 'appease.' Your father wanted you to appease me."

"Yeah, that's right. And what's he gonna do if I don't?"

"Send someone else?" Euphrene asked hopefully.

"Nuh-uh. He ain't. And you wanna know for why? Because I'm the last kid left! He'll prolly just send all his horses and all his men."

"For me to eat?"

"Nah, he likes them. He don't like kids, but his horses—boy, he *loves* them things."

"I can understand that," said the knight, patting the neck of his snow-white steed.

"Nope," continued the child, "Pop'll probably just run ya out of the kingdom. Shove ya off onto somebody else. Let them feed ya for a change."

"I wouldn't mind that," said Euphrene, brightening up. "I've always wanted to travel. And I do need to start accumulating gold at some point. Poor dragons don't attract the best mates. You've got to have some capital—that's what my mother says. A little nest egg."

"Gold?" repeated the knight. "If you like gold, we might be able to work out a deal."

Euphrene knew full well that humans aren't to be trusted. But when the subject of gold comes up, even the wisest dragon can be tempted.

"What did you have in mind?" she asked.

"Well, see here," said the knight seriously. "I've got to convert these pagans here in Libya to Christianity. The job's got to be done, and I'm just the guy to do it."

"All right," said Euphrene.

"S'all right by me, too," said the child, "if there's blood. Will there be ravenous lions?"

"No."

"How 'bout ax-wielding gladiators in combat to the death?"

"No," replied the knight. "But there might be dragons."

"Huh," grunted the child, unimpressed.

"Where does the, um, gold come in?" said Euphrene, returning to the key point.

"I have a sack full of gold right here," said the knight, pointing to a bulging leather bag almost as big as himself that was slung across his horse's back. "I'd be happy to give it to you. I don't really need it. I'm working for the cause."

Euphrene reached out a delicate claw. "Well, that's very kind of you, sir knight."

"Oh, you can call me George," replied the knight. He patted the bag, and the coins clinked invitingly. "It's a big bag, isn't it? And terribly heavy. I don't see how you could possibly carry it."

"Don't worry about that," Euphrene assured him. "Dragons have a special stomach just for carrying gold. It's how we transport our hoard when we move house."

"That's convenient, isn't it? As I say, I don't really need this gold. But it does have sentimental value. It's the last thing my sainted father gave me before he passed over, God rest his soul. And before I part with this precious souvenir of the past, I would like to ask a little favor."

"Of course," replied our kindly heroine. "Anything I can do."

"Well, it's so minor that I scarcely like to mention it, but I do have a job to do. And converting the heathen is a real challenge, let me tell you! I'm not sure why, but they don't seem to like being converted. They'll do anything to get out of it. They run and hide; they throw things. It's like I'm asking them to take a bath or something. Anyway, you and I could make things a lot easier on everybody if we could work a little ruse, a little subterfuge."

"Wha's a super-fudge?" asked the child. She had been following the conversation with great interest, while blowing and popping enormous bubbles of a color that matched her sparkly gown.

"A subterfuge, your pink-ness, is a ploy or stratagem by which you convince the other party of a thing that is not true."

"Oh, you gonna trick 'em."

"Yes, my dear. For their own good, of course."

"What kinda trick you gonna pull, mister?"

"Ah! Now this is where our good friend the dragon comes in. If I bring this huge dragon, breathing fire all over the place, into the middle of town, everyone will be frightened, won't they?"

The child guffawed as she envisioned this cheerful scene. "Sure! They'll pee their pants! They'll yell and scream and run around like headless chickens!"

"But what if I said I'd kill the dragon for them, if they converted to Christianity? What do you think they'd do?"

The child chewed on her plastic wand as she considered this complex question. "Yeah, ya got somethin' there, mister. I reckon they'd do 'most anything to get ridda that dragon."

Euphrene was loath to dampen their pretty enthusiasm, however she felt she had to point out the flaw in the plan. "But I don't want to be killed, even to oblige you, Sir George. Even for such a nice big bag of gold."

"No, no, this is where the subterfuge comes in. Once they've converted, I'll lead you out of town, telling the good citizens that I'm going to kill you, you see? Then you can fly off wherever you want."

"With the gold," added Euphrene, just to clarify things.

"Absolutely. With, as you say, the gold."

"But where's the blood?" demanded the child. "If ya don't kill it, there won't be any."

"We'll have our subterfuge. It will be such a funny joke—ha ha ha!"

The child thought for a moment, then nodded in approval. "I'd like to see my pop's face when ya show up with a dragon, breathing fire all over the place. Yeah, that'll be some fun."

Euphrene looked at the plan from all sides and could see no flaw in it. She got her gold, and these lower creatures got to play their peculiar games.

"I'm willing," she said. "How do we begin?"

"Well," said the knight, "I suppose we have to make it look like you are under my control. Do you have a leash? Or a chain, perhaps?"

"I'm afraid not," said Euphrene, who seldom wore jewelry.

"The princess has a sash," the knight pointed out. "We can use that."

The child, eager to see the fun that had been promised her, quickly unwound the long pink sash that had kept her dress from dragging in the mud. Sir George tied the sash around Euphrene's neck and, with the knight holding on to the loose end of it, they started off toward the distant city of Silene.

As it turned out, the child was not just a princess but also a prophet. As they approached the city walls, the inhabitants immediately began yelling and screaming. The knight suggested to Euphrene that a little fire might help move things along. She blew a couple of gentle puffs, and the townsfolk stumbled over each other to make way for the knight and dragon as they squeezed through the city gate.

The child was having the time of her life. She pointed and laughed until her eyes watered and her nose ran. The humans did in fact look just like headless chickens—so much so that Euphrene started to feel hungry. But she distracted herself by watching to see if any of the running figures happened to drop any gold.

She was only able to lap up some small change, however, before they reached the gates of the castle. The king, clutching his head, was visible in one of the upper windows—perfectly placed to hear the knight as he announced in a loud voice, "Good people of Silene! I, George of Lydda, have captured this fearsome beast and have come to present it to your king."

No one clapped. This was hardly surprising, since the knight, the child, and Euphrene were by now completely alone in the street.

"But," continued George, as if a new thought had struck him, "I would be happy to dispatch the dragon for you, if you'd prefer."

"Yes, yes," came a gasping voice from the upper floor of the palace. "Thanks so much, but we really don't have the, um, space for any more dragons. Trying to declutter. You know how it is."

The child, hidden behind Euphrene, hugged herself and sputtered with laughter.

"So, you'd like me to take it away, then?" asked the knight.

"Yes, please," said the king, sounding relieved.

"And when I return," said George, "we can discuss your conversion to Christianity."

"Christianity!" said the king. "Of course! We've been meaning to convert for ages. But you know how it is. Always so busy. First one thing, then another. Ha ha!"

"Then I shall take the dragon out to the coast and kill it immediately," declared the knight. "All I need is a big bag so I can bring you back its head."

"A bag! A bag!" the king cried eagerly. "Someone bring this knight a bag!"

A moment later a page appeared with a cloth sack, and the knight and Euphrene turned and made their way back through the empty streets to the rocky shore of the Mediterranean.

"You see how easy that was?" said the knight, untying the pink sash from around Euphrene's neck. "No trouble at all. Now you can go wherever you want. Feels like a nice tailwind springing up."

"Oh, very easy," agreed Euphrene. "I hardly feel that I have earned that bag of gold. But since you were so kind as to offer it…"

"The gold!" cried George. "I'll forget my head next. Yes, here it is." He lifted the leather bag and assisted Euphrene to cram it between her jaws. It was certainly a nice size, though not quite as heavy as she had expected.

Euphrene extended her wings and, with a wave at the knight, let the wind lift her up into the air. As she banked and headed north, she tipped her snout up and felt the bag slither down her throat. Just as it was passing out of her esophagus and into her stomach, she heard a faint, triumphant voice.

"Told ya you were gonna eat me!"

Euphrene was horrified. She opened her jaws wide and coughed, hoping to disgorge the bag and its disgusting occupant into the sea over which she was flying. Unfortunately, the bag had passed completely into her stomach. Not the gold stomach, because her body was smart enough to know the difference between metal and meat. It went into her digestive stomach. And, though that stomach was lined with iron like the stomachs of all dragons, it had never had to cope with anything as appalling as the princess Ringarosy.

By this time, Euphrene was approaching Sicily. She considered setting down and finding an alchemist to make her an emetic, but she had set her heart on visiting Germany. Her mother had told her there were lots of nice little towns there where the streets were paved with gold just waiting to be collected, and that many German chieftains buried hoards of gold specifically for dragons to find. So she continued north.

Euphrene was feeling very sorry for herself. Not only had she been cheated out of the gold coins the knight had promised her, but she'd been forced to eat this unsanitary child. Soon her stomach began to feel the effects. It twisted itself into knots and made all sorts of gurgling noises. A few miles later and the pain became severe. Over central Italy, Euphrene started to run a temperature. Her wings were shaking. She realized she was in no condition to continue her journey, and looked for somewhere to land.

Her mother had told her much about the glories of Rome, so she was pleased to see that huge city appear beneath her. But as she drifted closer, it seemed that Rome was not what it used to be. Her mother, who had toured the city several hundred years before, had spoken of white marble temples, gold-domed palaces, and streets crowded with harpies and centaurs. But all the buildings Euphrene could see looked deserted. Ivy grew over the ruins of the temples. There were gaping holes in the earth where the surface had collapsed and exposed the catacombs beneath. Rome seemed like a ghost town.

But Euphrene was in no condition to be choosy. At the moment, the holes looked tremendously inviting. Into one of the biggest ones she eased herself and her painful stomach. Though a tight fit, the catacombs were pleasantly dark and quiet. They had a moist dankness about them that Euphrene found soothing. Pushing aside a few sarcophagi engraved with names like *J. Avita Mamaea* and *P. Cornelius Tacitus*, she stretched out full-length along one of the larger tunnels.

Euphrene tried to relax, for she knew that stress exacerbates gastroenteritis, but relaxing was next to impossible. Her stomach was bloated and she suffered terribly from gas. Releasing it into the catacombs helped a little. She fluttered her wings to refresh the air, since the gas had a faint odor that made her new home a bit stuffy. In this way, she acquired some relief.

But as soon as she began to feel a little better and tried to get up, a new twinge would take her, and she was forced to lie down again.

She spent three days in this sort of misery, wondering if she would ever recover. On the fourth day she was sighing over her uncomfortable condition when the gleam of torches attracted her attention. By their light, she beheld an elderly man approaching, dressed in jeweled robes and a tall hat. Following him, at a respectful distance, were several attendants carrying fans and incense burners, and a positive crowd of armed men with helmets and spears.

"Ho!" called one of the attendants. "Arise, monster! Can you not see that Pope Silvester approaches?"

"The pope," exclaimed Euphrene, awestruck. "Well, my goodness!" Only a few days in Rome and she was already moving in the highest circles! Her mother would be so pleased. "I do apologize for not rising, Your Holiness. I'm afraid I am a trifle indisposed."

"Is that so?" said the elderly man, grimacing and raising a perfumed handkerchief to his nose. "That's too bad. We were hoping that our deputation would be able to encourage you to shorten your stay in our fair city. Your, shall we say, *fragrance* has caused the demise of hundreds of our citizens, and hundreds more hover at death's door."

"How embarrassing," murmured Euphrene, blushing to the roots of her purple scales.

"There are so many charming tourist spots in Italy," continued the old man. "Many even more attractive than Rome. You might enjoy the beaches of Naples, for example, or the romantic canals of Venice. Lake Como, also, is very pleasant this time of year."

"That does sound appealing," agreed Euphrene. "But right now I'm not sure I can move at all."

"What seems to be the trouble?" said the old gentleman.

"A minor stomach ailment, Holy Father," replied Euphrene. She felt it would be indelicate to tell him that she had eaten someone who had disagreed with her.

"Ah! You suffer the same malady as myself! Is it like a stabbing pain in the middle of your chest?"

"No, mine is more of a throbbing sensation on the right side. Just here, under my wing."

"Does it get worse at night, and then come on again suddenly first thing in the morning?"

"Yes! Exactly like that!"

"Does the extract of the birch tree help at all? Or peppermint?"

"I haven't tried either of those," admitted Euphrene. "You see, my affliction came upon me quite suddenly, and I have not had an opportunity to attempt any physic."

"Well, I have an excellent physician, and I can get him to make you up the same tonic he makes me. Works like a charm."

"That is so very kind of you," said Euphrene, pleased to have met such a compassionate human.

"And after you have taken a dose, we could perhaps resume our discussions on travel?"

"I would enjoy that," said Euphrene with a sigh.

Bidding her good day, Pope Silvester and his armed guard withdrew.

The pope was as good as his word, and in a few hours a dozen doctors in black robes appeared bearing a huge cup full of a thick red liquid that smelled like cherries.

"What a spectacular goblet! It looks like gold." Euphrene's eyes shone. Just looking at the cup made her feel better. "And are those emeralds on the sides?"

"The pope thought you would like it," said the head doctor, a man with a long black beard and an odd, fixed smile.

Euphrene put her snout close to the soft, glowing surface of the golden chalice and watched the torchlight glitter on the green stones. "Is it a gift? Can I keep it?"

"Of course! It's all yours! The goblet, and this delicious tonic. One dose and all your troubles will end. You just drink it all down like a good dragon."

His manner was condescending, like that of all doctors. Ordinarily, Euphrene would have challenged him on it, but at the moment she was in too much pain. She opened her jaws and tossed the entire chalice down her throat, where her digestive system took over and guided the chalice into her gold stomach and the tonic to her digestive stomach. She grimaced at the taste, which seemed a little heavy on the artificial cherry flavoring.

The black-bearded doctor watched her and chuckled in a friendly way. The other doctors standing behind him chuckled, too. And then they laughed. And suddenly the laughter was not so friendly anymore.

"Ha ha ha!" cried the head doctor. "A gift! Our gift to you! Pope Silvester's curse be upon you and all your kind, evil worm. For the liquid was *POISON!* Ha ha ha!"

"Ha ha ha!" echoed the other doctors.

"And soon," said doctor black beard, "you'll be *writhing in agony!*"

As they laughed, the doctors looked expectantly at Euphrene.

"You'll be dissolved from the inside out!"

Euphrene gazed back in horror.

"There will be nothing left of you but scales and bones! Soon! Any minute now you'll start to feel the shooting pains. Any... minute... now!"

But Euphrene did not feel any shooting pains. In fact, she felt no pain at all. The poison had done what nothing else could have: it had finally corroded the indigestible remains of the Libyan princess. It had even dissolved her non-biodegradable pink plastic wand. But Rome, they tell us, is the city of miracles.

Euphrene sat up and glared down at the doctors, who had by now stopped laughing.

"Did you call me a *worm?*" she demanded. "Is that what you just said? I have *never* been so insulted in all my life! I will certainly not stay where I'm not wanted."

With a last fiery belch, she burned the doctors to a crisp. She then took her departure from Rome, pausing only long enough to consume ten of the roast physicians. Euphrene hadn't eaten anything in four days, and she needed the extra calories to get her to Germany.

Once in the air, Euphrene got her bearings and headed north again. Soon she was passing over the Alps, where she could admire her reflection in the many placid lakes. And on the other side of the mountains, here it was at last—Germany.

Euphrene inhaled deeply and immediately scented gold. She let her nose lead her first to Munich, then to Regensburg, Bamberg, and all the other burgs. She found no precious metals lying in the streets, but discovered three nice little collections of treasure that had been buried and deserted, just as her mother had told her. She obtained additional gold from several local princes, whose wooden castles burned nicely and gave the cool air that lovely smoky fragrance that is so pleasant in early autumn.

By the time Euphrene reached Denmark, she had a nice little hoard packed into her gold stomach, one that would do credit to any young dragon.

After careful deliberation, she decided it was finally time to settle down. Her goal was a nice, cozy little cave somewhere, where she could display her collection. It could be underground or above, but it had to have enough square footage for a bed made up of all her loose change.

She looked around and finally found what seemed to be the perfect spot. In Sweden, on the edge of Lake Vänern, was a high stone cliff with a cleft that led into a big, dry cave with high ceilings. The view over the lake was quite spectacular. And after Euphrene had arranged every piece of her hoard to her liking, she looked forward to a wonderful life, enjoying all the benefits of Sweden with its low-cost education and excellent healthcare system.

Unfortunately, no one had warned her about the crime rate.

Euphrene felt so secure in her new home that she took no precautions at all to protect her valuables when she went out. One day, a local wandered in and absconded with the prize of her collection—the chalice that Pope Silvester had given her in Rome. Euphrene gave chase, but lost the man on the edge of a nearby village. She was forced to set fire to several buildings before the village chief would come out and discuss the matter.

"I don't know what you mean," he said stiffly. "We Geats are a noble people. No one from my village would steal a gold chalice."

This was so clearly a lie that Euphrene had to burn down a bit more of the village and the surrounding barns and crops.

"Yes, yes," admitted the chief finally, his pale skin growing paler. "I remember now. We do have a gold chalice with emeralds on it. But it belongs to my wife. She, um, uses it for mixing glögg. Had it for ages. An old family heirloom."

His lies convinced Euphrene that he was not worthy to be the chief of a village. When she was finished, there was nothing left for him to be chief of.

She returned home and tried to take pleasure in all her other lovely treasures, like the heavy gold collar and the huge serving dish with the bulls' heads around the edge. But it just wasn't the same.

A few days later, Euphrene was rearranging her treasures, trying to cover the hole where the goblet had been, when she heard a loud voice outside her cave.

"Hey! Hey, youse!"

Euphrene looked out. On the path in front of the cave stood a stocky old man with long, ratty hair and a drooping mustache. He wore armor and a helmet and what looked like a fur coat slung over his back.

"I beg your pardon," said Euphrene coldly, for she despised rudeness. "Were you addressing me, sir?"

"Yer damn straight," replied the individual. "I gotta bone to pick with you, serpent."

"A bone?"

"Yeah. Say, what do you wanna go burning down the whole country for? Everybody's longhouses and cattle cooked to a crisp. It makes a mess, see? And then my thegns and earls come running to me. Expecting me to fix everything, just cuz I'm the king."

"The king!" Euphrene drew back. In spite of herself, she was impressed. *First knights,* she thought, *then popes, and now a king!* She seemed destined to move in high society.

"Sure! Don'cha know who I am? I'm King Beowulf, the boss of this here territory. And what I say is, it's all wrong to bust up the joint like that. Fifty years I spent gettin' my kingdom all nice and jake. And just when I think I can sit back and take a load off, all these barbarians and bishops and dragons come swanking in and—"

"But if you're the king, you should be on my side," urged Euphrene. "They stole my jeweled goblet, the one Pope Silvester gave me. I was only trying to recover my own property."

"Goblet, eh? You mean this little trinket?" The king pulled the goblet out of the pocket of his fur coat.

"Oh, yes, thank you for returning it," said Euphrene, stretching out a paw.

"Say, don't get fresh with me, serpent. The pope? The pope in Rome gave *you* a golden goblet? That's a hot one. Come clean, monster. You stole it, din'cha?"

Euphrene drew herself up to her full height.

"Are you calling me a liar, sir?" she demanded.

"Yeah, I'm callin' you a liar. A liar and a thief. Come on out and take what's coming to you. Nice and easy, now. I've got you covered." He drew a heavy sword from its scabbard and waved it around menacingly.

Euphrene was becoming a little annoyed at this crude old man. A few fireballs escaped her nostrils, but she tried to remain calm and reason with the villain.

"You really shouldn't come to people's homes and threaten them with swords," she chided him. "I may only be seven hundred years old, but my mother taught me how to take care of myself."

"Yah! I ain't afraid of no monster. I've killed plenty of scum like you. I'll give it to ya, but good. Come on out and make it snappy. I wanna see the color of yer insides."

Now, even the most calm and peace-loving dragon can lose her temper once in a while. Euphrene had her pride, and being called a rat, a monster, and scum was the last straw. She unsheathed her claws and walked out of the cave toward the king, intending to teach him a few manners.

The king immediately swung his sword at her. "Take that!" he cried. "And that!"

The sword did little harm to Euphrene. It merely bounced off her adamantine scales. Seeing how weak the poor old king was, Euphrene decided to just wait until his exertions had tired him out and made him more reasonable.

But the king continued to hack away at Euphrene until suddenly his sword bounded back so violently that it sliced right through the chain mail covering his chest. He dropped his sword and clutched at the wound, which was bleeding freely.

"And that," said Euphrene, "will, I hope, be a lesson to you..."

But before she could properly explain this lesson—a lesson that might have been extremely helpful to the king during the rest of his very short life—another warrior appeared, catching the king as he slumped to the ground.

"My lord!" he cried.

The king gave a couple of coughs and clutched at the newcomer's arm. "Wiglaf? Is that you?"

"Yes, O king, it is I, Wiglaf, most loyal of all your retainers."

"I'm all washed up, Wiglaf. This looks like the end fer me."

"Oh, say not so, most noble lord!"

"I can't hold out much longer," said the king. He gulped dramatically and reached one hand toward the sky as a dozen more warriors made their entrance from behind a nearby hill. "Oh! Everything's gettin' dark. I can't see. Don't leave me, Wiglaf! It's gettin' dark... dark... Goodbye, old pal. Goodbye..."

By now, a hundred or so armed men had gathered in front of Euphrene's cave. They looked from their dead king to Euphrene in an unpleasant manner.

"The beast has slain our liege lord," cried the one called Wiglaf, jumping to his feet. "We must take our revenge and destroy the serpent who has robbed us of the flower of heroic-ness that was King Beowulf of the Geats."

The men produced an array of swords, spears, and other pointed weapons, and Euphrene realized that her cave would never be the quiet, comfortable retreat she had hoped. She dashed back inside and gulped down all the gold within her reach. Then, getting a running start, she sprinted past the warriors and was high in the afternoon sky before they could organize their attack.

With several graceful flaps of her purple wings, Euphrene left Geatland behind her.

But she was in the air without a plan. She seethed with anger over the king's insults and the loss of her beautiful golden chalice. Why was it that humans were just so—well, rude, ungrateful, unprincipled, deaf, stubborn, smelly? The list just went on and on.

She decided that, in her current state, what she really needed was a sympathetic ear. Someone who would understand her pain.

Luckily, she remembered that one of her father's relatives lived in the area, so she turned and headed out to sea, deep into the territory of the World Ocean. She would go talk to old Jörmungandr, the world-encircling serpent.

Although it is easy to tell where Jörmungandr is, he being the dragon who surrounds the entire world, it can be a challenge to figure out where he *is*—that is, where to find the part you can converse with. Euphrene had to fly far out to sea before she spotted his gigantic horn sticking up out of the water.

There not being any other solid place to set down, she landed on the horn. Immediately, the ocean around her began to churn. A massive goat-like head with a long, silky beard rose up out of the water.

"Who dithturbth the thleep of the mighty Jörmungandr?" bellowed a deep voice.

"Hello, Uncle," called our heroine. "It is Euphrene, Typhon's daughter."

"Ah, little Euphrene!" Jörmungandr's whole goat face brightened. "Thorry I yelled at you. I thought you were Thor. What bringth you here? Thorry if it'th a little hard to underthtand me. I'th got to keep my tail in my mouth or the whole world will fall apart. You know how it ith."

"Yes, I quite understand," replied Euphrene. "I was in the neighborhood, and I thought I'd drop by. I hope you don't mind."

"That was very thoughtful!" said the leviathan, moving his tail to the other side of his mouth to assist communication. "You've grown since the last time I saw you. How's your father? How's your hoard coming along? Have you found a nice cave yet?"

"Oh, Uncle, that's just the trouble. I'm working very hard to amass my hoard, but there are so many *humans* all over the place, and they're so mean to me. They cheat me and steal my gold and call me names. It's just terrible!"

"There, there," said Jörmungandr. "I've heard that humans can be difficult. But that's nothing compared to the gods! You can't imagine how badly they treat me."

"You, Uncle? But you're the great Jörmungandr!"

"And you would think that, as World Serpent, I would be entitled to a little respect, wouldn't you? But look at this! Just look at this cut on my lip."

"That's a nasty wound," declared Euphrene.

"Thor did that just last week. He came out fishing with some buddies and threw an ox head into the water. I thought he'd brought me a present, but *NO!* It was attached to a fishing line! He thought he'd just reel me in, like I'm some little trout. But I'll get my revenge." Jörmungandr's fins began to twitch, causing enormous whirlpools to form behind his head. "Any minute now he'll be back, and then he'll see what a sea serpent can really do. Thinks he's so smart. Him and his toy hammer. I'll snap him in two."

"Wouldn't you have to let go of your tail to do that?"

"I suppose I would. Thor can be a handful when he's riled up."

"But the world would be destroyed, Uncle!"

"Yes, I expect the moon and sun will go out. And all the stars, of course. And the mountains will topple. And the sea will probably drown the land. But it can't be helped. It's gone beyond insults now." Jörmungandr waggled his white beard and flashed his yellow eyes dangerously. "He's disfigured my beautiful face. I can't let him get away with that."

He blinked a massive eye at Euphrene. "Well, my dear girl, I can't keep you here chatting. Thor will be along at any moment, and I wouldn't want a nice little dragon like you to witness the damage I'm going to inflict on that guy. You just get along home now and work on that hoard of yours."

"But that's just it, Uncle! My hoard is so small. And I have no home! No matter where I go, I'm driven away. No one wants me!"

"Now, don't say that, my dear. Don't say that. In fact, if you want a job, I heard there's someone who's desperate to hire a dragon."

"Really?" Euphrene rubbed the tears from her eyes. "I hadn't thought about getting a job."

"Yes. And they're willing to pay in gold."

"That sounds wonderful," said Euphrene, perking up immediately. "Who is it? How do I get in touch with them? Do I need a résumé? Because I don't have much work experience."

"You can use me as a reference," said Jörmungandr. "Go to the Garden of the Hesperides and ask for Hera."

"Hera? The *goddess* Hera?"

"Yes. She's tough but fair. Usually. Anyway, it's worth a shot. Now go on, get out of here. And tell your father to call me once in a while!"

In spite of her concern over her uncle's wound, and his upcoming encounter with Thor, Euphrene's spirits rose as she made her way south again. With a job, she would feel like a real adult. A job that paid in gold was exactly what she needed to build her hoard. And working for a goddess—forget kings and popes—*that* was really starting at the top.

When she reached the Aegean Sea, she inquired about the location of Hera's garden from a passing flock of harpies. They tried to be helpful, but disagreed as to whether the garden was in Spain or Morocco.

"Head west," they all advised her. "And then ask again."

At the Straits of Gibraltar, Euphrene finally got proper directions from a nine-headed hydra. She arrived at the garden of the Nymphs of Twilight at, well, twilight. The Hesperides were quite pleasant nymphs, and received Euphrene kindly. When they learned of her errand, they took her to the temple where Hera sat on her throne, surrounded by a noisy flock of peacocks.

Hera was a stern and imposing goddess wearing a golden crown atop a wavy perm. Euphrene prostrated herself before Hera's throne, terrified to face a goddess who radiated such power and efficiency.

Hera gazed down at Euphrene with a critical eye. "Typhon's daughter, eh?"

"Yes, O queen most high."

"Well, Jörmungandr speaks well of you, and you look like a strong young dragon. I need someone to protect the tree that grows my golden apples. I'll give you one golden apple for every thirty days you remain in my employment, payable at autumn harvest. After a probationary period, of course. Do you think you could handle the work?"

"Oh, yes, ma'am. I'm sure I could." Twelve golden apples a year! Euphrene was thrilled.

"You'd better think about it before you commit," warned the goddess. "I've got a good-for-nothing stepson called Heracles who's nothing but trouble. I just heard through the grapevine that he's been boasting he can steal my apples. He's a pretty tough customer."

"Well, so am I, ma'am," replied Euphrene, who was not about to let some demigod get between herself and any golden apples.

Hera gave her a sharp look, but signed her up on a trial basis. After filling out several reams of HR paperwork, Euphrene was issued her badge and her health insurance card. And then her happy days at the Garden of the Hesperides began.

It was a pretty place. The extensive lawns were dotted with little groves of trees and white marble temples. Meals were provided as well. Hera refused to let Euphrene eat any of her peacocks, but there were plenty of swans and sheep, and no one complained about the occasional missing shepherd.

Hera gave her the use of a comfortable cave right next to the tree that produced the golden apples, so Euphrene could easily monitor the area. And since we all know that dragons can sleep with one eye open, Euphrene had no trouble shooing away the occasional bird or deer that approached the tree.

After their first interview, Euphrene saw little of Hera herself. The goddess' responsibilities as patron of marriage and childbirth took her all over the world. Any extra time was completely booked up with speaking engagements and a vlog tour for her most recent book, *What Did Zeus Ever Do For Me?* ("Edgy and thought-provoking."—*The L.A. Times*)

But the nymphs were good company, though a little empty-headed and frivolous. They spent their time singing and dancing and playing hopscotch across the lawns and through the orchards. And though Euphrene's job was not very taxing, she quickly realized why Hera had hired a dragon rather than letting the Hesperides guard the golden apples.

These apples were beautiful things. From the first, Euphrene loved them almost as much as Hera did. Her favorite pastime was to sit under the tree and count the apples as they sparkled in the light of the constantly setting sun. She was overjoyed when her probationary period was over and her earnings started. She was counting the hours until one of these spectacular pieces of fruit became hers. And she had to keep a close eye on the clock and make careful notes, because, being the Garden of Twilight, it was impossible to tell how much time had passed here just by looking at the sky.

In this way, several months went by. Under Euphrene's care, hundreds of new buds bloomed, grew into red fruit, and began to harden into solid gold apples. By her calculations, she was owed two and three-quarter golden apples when the worst happened. Hera's stepson arrived for a visit.

Euphrene saw at once why Hera disliked him. He was a big, savage brute, hideous to look at, with glaring eyes and a scowling face. For clothing he wore nothing but the skin of an enormous lion. As an accessory he dragged around a huge wooden club, Neanderthal style. Shaving appeared to be a foreign concept. He looked, in short, like the kind of individual no mythological creature would care to meet down a dark alley.

But the nymphs were crazy about him. They plied him with wine and got him drunk enough to join in their boisterous games. They flirted shamelessly, competing to see which could hold his attention the longest. When they were alone with Euphrene, they even talked of marriage.

"He'd be a catch," they told her. "He's Zeus' son. I wouldn't mind living in a little villa on Mount Olympus with him. Which of us do you think he likes best?"

In Euphrene's opinion, Heracles didn't know one of the Hesperides from the other. She watched him closely and thought that his eyes strayed more often to the tree with the golden apples than to the nymphs. She didn't bother telling the nymphs, but she knew that if Heracles could get his hands on some apples he'd be off without giving the nymphs a second thought.

One evening the Hesperides appeared with their wine jugs and plates of baklava, just as silly and giggly as usual, with Heracles in tow.

"Have a drink, Herc," said one of the nymphs, "and then let's get back to our game of Twister."

"Lawdy, honey," drawled Heracles. "Y'all ha' got me plum tuckered out. Let's set a spell. Why don't you get out that lil' ole ukulele of yorn and give us a tune?"

"Of course! Anything you want."

TALES FOR YOUNG DRAGONS

And they started in on one of Euphrene's favorites, the old song about the bloody battle between the lion and the bull. The Hesperides had lovely, soothing voices, and by the twenty-fourth verse Euphrene was fast asleep.

When she awoke and stretched her wings, Heracles and the Hesperides were gone. And they weren't the only ones—six of the golden apples were also missing.

Euphrene counted the apples three times, telling herself not to panic. She searched the ground around the tree. She searched the lawn for many yards in each direction. But the apples had not fallen off or rolled away. They had just disappeared.

As if sensing her loss, Hera herself appeared in a blaze of light, still wearing the pinstripe suit and string of pearls from her last TV appearance. Her eyes blazed like hot coals. In fact, they were shooting sparks.

"Dragon!" she cried, tapping one patent-leather pump. "Where are my apples?"

Euphrene groveled. "They were right here a minute ago, your majestic-ness. I counted them before the nymphs arrived. But they put me to sleep with their singing. Heracles must have taken them."

"Sleep?" thundered Hera. "I hired you to watch that tree, not to sleep!"

"But the nymphs—"

"Don't blame others for your mistakes! You've got to take responsibility!"

Euphrene slumped. "Yes, I know. I'm sorry."

Her penitence did not appease Hera. "I won't have incompetent guards on my staff!" she shouted. "You're fired! Go clean out your desk immediately!"

"Very well," sighed Euphrene. "I suppose two golden apples is better than none."

195

"Two? Two golden apples? Do you think I'd give a single one of my valuable apples to such a miserable excuse for a fire lizard?"

But Euphrene stood her ground. "You promised," she reminded Hera. "You said after the probationary period I was to have one apple for each thirty days, and I've been here eighty-one days. I've been keeping count."

Hera smiled nastily. "Really? Has the sun ever risen or set? How many 'days' have you actually been here?"

Euphrene's jaw dropped. "That's *cheating!*" she exclaimed. "You're trying to cheat me out of my salary."

"I'm a goddess," said Hera smugly. "My universe, my rules. Now get out of my garden before I do something you'll regret."

"You... You can't get away with this! I'm going to my uncle. Then we'll see whose universe it is."

Euphrene spread her wings and rose up into the sky.

Hera can't treat me like this, she said to herself. *I'll go back to the World Ocean and get Uncle Jörmungandr to petition the divine court on my behalf.*

A moment later a painful blow landed on her back. Looking down, she saw a golden apple falling back to earth and Hera in the act of picking another off the tree. The goddess aimed the apple right at Euphrene and let fly, connecting this time with Euphrene's shoulder. The goddess had a powerful pitching arm, and already Euphrene could feel bruises forming beneath her purple scales.

As she watched, Hera plucked three more apples and sent them after the first two. Euphrene climbed a bit higher, but still couldn't escape the agonizing bombardment of metal fruit.

Suddenly afraid that Hera would hit one of her wings, Euphrene strained her muscles to their utmost. She shot straight up into the night sky. The air grew thinner, and the stars bigger and brighter. But still Hera's apples struck with deadly accuracy.

By now, Euphrene was beginning to tire. She was just wondering whether she'd better go back and beg Hera for forgiveness when her snout suddenly slammed against something solid. She could see nothing, but, reaching out a claw, she heard a loud *clink*.

She realized now just how far she had come—she had run straight into the revolving crystalline sphere to which the stars are attached.

Clutching her nose, she backed up a pace. All around her were the glittering stars she used to pine after, inset like enormous jewels into pockets carved in the crystal. It was an awesome sight.

A moment later she got another shock. A golden apple zipped past her ear, hit the crystal boundary, and stayed there. Hera had thrown it with such force that it had buried itself in the surface of the sphere.

At once, Euphrene knew what she had to do.

She flapped against the invisible surface as if she were frantic to escape. But she kept an eye on Hera, and on the apples speeding toward her. She twisted and turned to make sure all the apples hit the sphere and not her. In this way, giggling a good deal to herself, Euphrene watched fifty or so golden apples become permanently fixed to the sphere of heaven.

All of a sudden, Hera realized that her apples were not coming back down to her. She shook her fists at Euphrene and shouted something the dragon could not hear. Then she stomped off back to her temple to change her shoes, which were pinching her feet.

Euphrene settled down onto the under-surface of heaven and surveyed her new hoard. So many gold apples glowing in the dazzling light of the stars! It was a hoard like no other dragon had ever possessed in the whole course of draconian history. And so she decided to stay there.

Of course, she lived happily ever after.

And if you go outside on a starry night and look directly north, you can see her in the sky today. Her beautiful name, Euphrene, has long been forgotten. Now they just call her Draco, the dragon. But from her crystal cave high above, in the midst of her golden treasure, Euphrene still gazes down upon each and every dragon.

Let her example inspire and guide you as you strive to amass the hoard of your dreams.

Extract from the Richmond Herald's Review of Books, *August 15, 2024:*

"*...and as for* Tales for Young Dragons, *I've never read such drivel in my life. It's just not possible for this dragon to have met St. George of Lydda, who was beheaded by the Roman army in 303 A.D., and then immediately encounter Sylvester I, who wouldn't even become pope until 314 A.D.! The dragon that St. George killed in Libya to free the princess was obviously a completely different dragon from the one spreading the plague throughout Rome with its breath that Pope Sylvester defeated a decade later. And then the most glaring error of all—putting St. George and Pope Sylvester in the time of Beowulf, who was king in Geatland the 500s. Ridiculous! It is true that a dragon did terrorize southern Sweden after a thief stole a golden cup from its hoard. But Beowulf slew that beast with his dagger. Note that history is* very clear *that these dragons* did not survive. *Where this author gets her facts, I cannot imagine!*"

Author Biographies

Valerie Brown is a published short story and micro-fiction author. Her work has appeared in literary forums such as *101 Words, Paragraph Planet, Fark Fiction's 2018 Anthology*, and *The Opening Line Literary 'Zine*. For updates on her current projects and for photos of her hectic life as a mom of spirited two-leggeds and furry four-leggeds, follow her on Instagram @vedbrown.

Ivy Hamid is a middle-grade fantasy writer whose most recent manuscript was a finalist in the 2022 London Times/Chicken House Children's Fiction Competition and James River Writers' Best Unpublished Novel competition for 2023. She was an artsy kid who got a degree in art history, and has worked in and around museums ever since. She put in her time in New York, slightly to the south of Sing Sing, before moving down to the real South. She belongs to the James River Writers and the Society for Children's Book Writers and Illustrators. *Tales for Young Dragons* received an honorable mention in the Writers of the Future competition in 2023.

Renée A. Hill, retired, was an Associate Professor of Philosophy who taught at Virginia State University for twenty years. Her area of specialization was Political Philosophy and her research interests centered around justice and fairness. Hill was Co-Director of the Institute for the Study of Race Relations at VSU for twelve years and is on the board of the Southern Initiative Algebra Project. She is trained in conflict resolution and techniques for healing trauma in communities, and volunteered in the Mindfulness Room at the Martin Luther King, Jr Middle School in Richmond, VA. Most importantly, she loves fantasy. A member of the Richmond Fantasy Collective, she spends her spare time reading and writing about beings with super-human abilities living in strange, new worlds.

Dean Radt received his MFA in Creative Writing from Lasell University's Solstice MFA program and was awarded the Dennis Lehane Fellowship for Fiction in 2020. His debut novel, the military fantasy *Trials of the Horseman*, was published in 2021. Dean is retired from a twenty-five-year career in public safety and is a member of James River Writers.

Kaitlyn Reeds grew up with a love of fantasy and animals. She earned her Wildlife Conservation degree from Virginia Tech where she caught, tagged, and handled live animals that regularly attempted to sink their teeth, fangs, or beaks into anything within reach. She includes her love of the outdoors and wildlife into her fantasy works. Kaitlyn currently lives in Virginia where she is a member of James River Writers and Richmond Fantasy Collective. When not writing, she is usually cuddling her cat, playing video games, or taking pictures of the birds in the backyard.

Follow the Richmond Fantasy Collective on Instagram @rfcwriters

Milton Keynes UK
Ingram Content Group UK Ltd.
UKHW031117080824
446563UK00006B/401